In Search of
a Distant Voice

by the same author
Strangers

In Search of
a Distant Voice

Taichi Yamada

Translated by Michael Emmerich

faber and faber

First published in the UK in 2006
by Faber and Faber Limited
3 Queen Square London WC1N 3AU

Originally published in Japan as Toku no koe wo sagashite,
by Shinchosha, Tokyo, in 1986

Typeset by Faber and Faber
Printed in England by Mackays of Chatham, plc

A CIP record for this book
is available from the British Library

ISBN 978-0571-22971-0
ISBN 0-571-22971-9

2 4 6 8 10 9 7 5 3 1

In Search of
a Distant Voice

1

Eight years ago, in Portland, Oregon, Kasama Tsuneo had wanted desperately to be normal. Everything that had happened in his life since then followed from that wish, though he couldn't exactly say he now had the kind of life he'd hoped for. It was true, though, that to this day he remained subjugated to that old desire.

It was in March last year that Tsuneo first experienced the phenomenon around which this tale will increasingly come to revolve.

Tsuneo got up at four-thirty in the morning. He was in the Ōtemachi Multi-Office Government Complex in Tokyo, in the rest station on the third floor of Building One. Four-thirty was pretty early, it's true, but that's how it goes. They had mornings like this four or five times a month. Three other men got out of their beds at the same time and started pulling on their shirts and pants. No one said a word. This silence didn't mean anything. They were tired, that's all.

Tsuneo fastened all the buttons on his pale-green patterned shirt, including the top one. He felt exposed when he left his collar open. He pulled on his dark-green corduroy pants. The knees were starting to wear out. His sweater was moss green. Tsuneo loved landscapes filled with green, though this wasn't the sort of thing a man of twenty-nine felt comfortable admitting. The overpowering green of the tropics.

Of course, you wouldn't find anything like that in this gray building. He had done what he could by sneaking in these little patches of the color . . . not that he thought this made people's lives any richer. He just figured green was a slight improvement over gray or navy blue, that's all.

Tsuneo put on his once-white sneakers. Every time he did this, it occurred to him that he needed to wash them. A well-washed pair of white sneakers makes you feel terrific. And yet he generally wore his out without even washing them once.

He pulled the strap of his holster, with his pistol inside, over his shoulder and tied its leather cord around his belt. Then he put on his black jacket.

The minibus carrying the four men pulled out of the building's underground parking lot at approximately five a.m.

It was still night outside, up above ground. A white glow without even a trace of warmth was just starting to bleed across the overcast sky; other than that it was dark. They took the Metropolitan Expressway as far as Iriya. Inspector Ōta drove while the three others had their breakfast of milk and bread.

Heavy clouds hung in the sky. Little by little, though, despite the bad weather, the dawn light revealed their surroundings.

As they turned off onto Nikkō Highway, a dozen or so crows fluttered up into the air from the roadside. You see this all the time in Tokyo, in the morning. There must be garbage scattered on the ground there, that's all. There's nothing ominous in their presence – of course not. 'Man, what the hell are you thinking?' Tsuneo smiled bitterly to himself, though his face remained expressionless. 'This job is so easy it's ridiculous even to tell myself these things.'

Once Tsuneo's thoughts reached this point, it usually occurred to him that talking silently to himself like this, conducting this internal back-and-forth, had become a sort of tic: it was something he did whenever he participated in a raid.

First he was overcome by a sense of foreboding. A second self would deny that feeling, dismissing it with a wry grin. Then he would realize that this back-and-forth was just part of the program. And then he would notice that even this realization itself was part of a ritual he had performed many hundreds of times. He was used to holding back his moods, keeping his feelings suppressed. Today, too, everything was happening as it always did.

'Hey, Ōta,' Tsuneo said, stepping into his role as supervisor. 'Why don't you let Sakuma take over?'

'I'm ready,' said Inspector Sakuma, half-rising in his seat.

'Don't forget, kid, this ain't no Corolla!' boomed Chief Inspector Miyazaki in his deep voice, as if he were criticizing Sakuma for an error he had made. He was only teasing, but the way he spoke made it sound like a reproach.

Last April, not long after he was transferred from the Narita office, Sakuma had driven the minibus headlong into a narrow alley, leaving them completely stuck. He had been chasing a Korean man. The Corolla Miyazaki referred to was Sakuma's own car.

'Afraid you'll have to get a new joke, Chief Inspector,' Sakuma replied, unfazed by the sharp edge in his boss's voice. 'I upgraded to a Mercedes ages ago.'

'Cheeky bastard!' Miyazaki burst out laughing. 'Sometimes a comeback can be *too* smart, you know.'

Tsuneo felt intimidated by Miyazaki's laugh, his booming voice. It sounded to him as though Miyazaki were trying to show he could be a better supervisor than him. Miyazaki was only a year younger than Tsuneo.

Ōta pulled over to the side of the road. He and Sakuma changed places. If they didn't switch fairly early on, Ōta would still be eating when they arrived.

'Full speed ahead!' Sakuma set the minibus in motion with another pointless aside. Tsuneo was intimidated by him too – this flippant twenty-three-year-old who seemed to have no idea that his boss was really his boss. And then there was the silent Ōta: who knew what was going on in his mind? It didn't help that Tsuneo felt this way toward them, though, that was for sure. They were very able subordinates, all three of them. As an Assistant Security Officer, it wasn't all that often that Tsuneo got to supervise a raid. Most often one of the Security Officers – or if it was a particularly important case, the Chief Security Officer or even the Chief of Security himself – would take the lead. On the one hand, then, Tsuneo felt genuinely happy to be setting out on this raid, with these three men. He could count on them being considerably more effective than other units. All three men had sterling reputations. From where he sat, all the way in the rear, Tsuneo could see the backs of their heads. Three men, all reliable. Ōta was taking a swig of milk, his mouth pressed against the paper carton. 'I suppose I could say I love these guys.' No way. But when he forced himself to whisper these words in his head, he began to think maybe he did feel that way, just a little. This was another step in his regular program of self-hypnosis. One by one, he had to suppress any feelings that might get in the way of his work.

The sense of foreboding, his timidity in the face of his own subordinates.

'Hey, Miyazaki.'

'Yes, sir!' Miyazaki replied without even turning around.

'You and Sakuma go in from the front, okay?'

'Sure,' Miyazaki replied, looking back this time.

'I'll go around the back with Ōta.'

'You got that, Ōta?' Miyazaki boomed again.

'Roger.'

'Hey, kid, it's not "Roger", it's "Yes, sir!" You can't do good work if you're trying to be cool all the time. Got it?'

'Got it.'

'It's not "Got it" either, kid. You say "Yes, sir!"'

'Yes, sir!'

After that, Miyazaki looked back at Tsuneo, a vulgar smirk on his lips. 'You need to take care of yourself, though, huh? Saitō was just saying that.'

'What are you talking about?' Tsuneo smiled dryly.

'Don't play innocent! The Director-General's been blabbing it all over the place. Too late to try and hide it now.'

Mr Saitō was Director-General of the General Affairs Division. Last month, he had been the formal matchmaker at a meeting between Tsuneo and a potential bride. Tsuneo and the woman – a credit union employee named Shibata Yoshie – were just beginning to develop a relationship.

'Got to look after that body of yours, huh?'

'Don't be a jerk.'

The minibus left Adachi ward and entered Sōka Town.

Tsuneo and Sakuma had scouted out the building they were headed for the previous day. Six Bangladeshi men were living together in a six-mat room on the first floor of a prefab apartment building. Tsuneo had taken the call one night when he was doing the graveyard shift. 'A neighbor' had turned them in. 'I just don't feel safe with people like them around,' a woman's voice had said. She didn't give her name or address or anything, but the Immigration Bureau takes these reports very seriously. The following day they went and checked the place out, and the morning after that – here they were. In a minibus rented from a private company, heading toward a raid. It was pretty clear that the men were in the country illegally.

Five minutes before six o'clock, the bus pulled up across from the apartment. By then it was daylight outside. Miyazaki immediately flung open the door; Tsuneo stepped out after him. There was a chill in the air. A few fields could still be seen here and there on either side of the two-lane road; off in the distance, there was a man on a bicycle, pedalling in their direction. There was no sign of anyone else.

Tsuneo cut across the street, quickly glancing back to confirm that Ōta was behind him. He stepped through a gate framed by two narrow posts and entered the yard, which was walled in by a low hedge; the moment he was inside, he headed around toward the back of the building. Sakuma would be leading the way in front, with Miyazaki following. Tsuneo and Ōta needed to be positioned outside the rear window by the time their partners arrived at their objective, the door.

To the rear of the apartment building, separated from it by a cinder-block wall, was a graveyard. Beyond the graveyard was a temple. Things could get complicated if anyone managed to get into the temple grounds, or the graveyard. They had to make sure no one got over that wall.

Sure enough, no sooner had Tsuneo set foot on the damp earth in back of the building than the window in front of him suddenly flew open. A man appeared with his foot on the windowsill, preparing to jump out.

'Don't move!' Tsuneo shouted in English, running toward the window. 'We're from Immigration!'

The foreigner, a young man with Indian features and large eyes, stood there with one foot on the windowsill, looking down at Tsuneo.

'We're from the Tokyo Regional Immigration Bureau!' Tsuneo repeated.

At last, he heard the sound of Miyazaki and Sakuma knocking on the door. How could this guy have figured out so soon that we were starting a raid? Of course, he had probably been on edge to begin with – to him, the noise of a minibus grinding to a halt in the early morning stillness and the sound of four pairs of sneakers crossing the street wouldn't have seemed particularly quiet.

'Open the door!' said Tsuneo to the man, still in English. 'We need to see your passports.'

'Okay,' said the man, nodding in apparent resignation.

The knocking continued.

'Opun za doa!' Ōta yelled out behind Tsuneo in his broken English.

Inside the dim room, another man moved, stood up, and headed for the door.

'Get your foot down!' Tsuneo shouted to the young man in front of him. 'Get your foot off the windowsill!'

'Okay.' The young man slowly removed his foot from the sill. He had slender legs; he was wearing jeans.

The door opened and Miyazaki walked into the apartment; the light streaming in behind him transformed his body into a silhouette. 'We're from the Tokyo Regional Immigration Bureau,' he said in Japanese. He said the same thing in English; then, as he removed his shoes, 'We'd like you to show us your passports' – this too was in English. He stepped up from the entryway into the room and stood there gazing down at the men sitting up on their futons.

There were eight of them. Not six. A second count confirmed this. Eight men living in a single six-mat room.

'You go in too, Ōta,' said Tsuneo. 'I'll be around in a second.'

'Yes sir.' Ōta headed for the front.

'There are eight of them,' Tsuneo called out.

'There sure are,' Sakuma called back, taking off his shoes. 'We hit the jackpot this time, huh?' The way he spoke, you'd think he'd just got more than his share of watermelon or something.

'Listen,' said Tsuneo in English to the man at the window. 'I want you to close the window and lock it.'

'Okay.' The young man didn't resist. He shut the window and started turning the locks.

Miyazaki was inspecting one of the men's passports. Tsuneo heard him talking in English through the glass. 'Yeah, your visa expired ages ago.'

Tsuneo kept watching the man on the other side of the window as he turned the locks. Finally he finished, and gestured with his right hand in Tsuneo's direction. *That's okay, right?*

Tsuneo nodded, then stepped back from the window to go around and give his partners a hand inside, since it seemed likely that all eight of them would have to go. Just then, his gaze landed on a large blue polyethylene garbage pail that was sitting right beside the cinderblock wall. The pail was directly in front of their window. That wasn't there yesterday, was it? And isn't it sort of strange to have a big polyethylene pail like that, one that's obviously meant to be used by the whole building, in a place so far away from the road? I can see why they'd want to keep it around the back, but still – it's odd. If you put your foot on that pail, it would be a cinch to get over the wall. Twenty or thirty seconds passed as these thoughts ran through Tsuneo's mind. He kept walking as he thought. He was considering these things, yes, but he didn't stop. He was just about to turn the corner of the building. That's how it always is when these things happen.

All of a sudden he heard the sound of the window opening behind him. By the time he spun around, the foreigner already had one foot on the pail.

'Stop!' Tsuneo shouted in English. But by then the young man was on the wall, and a moment later he had jumped across to the other side.

Tsuneo could hear Miyazaki bellowing in his rage.

'It's okay, it's okay! IT'S OKAY!' Tsuneo shouted, dashing back toward the window. 'I can handle this! Don't lose your head!' He was putting his foot on the pail as he said this. 'Don't let the others escape!' He leapt up onto the wall. He scanned the graveyard as he flew over, but saw no trace of the guy. He landed. The temple was approximately fifty meters away. Seeing how fast the young man had moved, it wasn't impossible that he had made a dash for the temple. He'd have to be almost superhuman to have made it, though. Within seconds of the young man jumping the fence, Tsuneo's eyes were scanning the graveyard. No matter how fast he'd run, Tsuneo should have got at least a momentary glimpse of his back as he scampered off. But the young man seemed to have disappeared, just like that.

'Come on out now,' Tsuneo said in English, running his eyes over the forest of gravestones. 'I know you're hiding.' He saw no sign of any movement. He slid his hand in under his jacket, across his chest, and touched his pistol. In the six years he'd been doing this job, he hadn't used it once. Of course he had no intention of using it now, either; it was just that the guy had gotten away so fast – it didn't seem possible. Who knows what he'd do if he were cornered? I'd lose if it came to a contest of strength. The threat posed by a pistol might come in handy.

Just then, Tsuneo heard the sound of very quiet breathing. A chill ran down his spine. He's close. Tsuneo took out his pistol. He must have hidden as soon as he jumped down. But why? Isn't it human nature to keep running, even if you can only make it a little farther away? This guy took the opposite tack, finding a hiding place immediately. *The man chasing me runs off into the distance. And while he's gone, I make my escape.* He's got guts if that's what he's thinking.

Already the sound had stopped. Tsuneo started inching slowly in the direction from which, for just a moment, he had sensed breathing. He crouched down, hiding in the shadow of a gravestone, and then, bit by bit, began looking out, widening his field of vision.

Two gravestones away, he caught a glimpse of the man's white shirt.

'I've got a gun,' Tsuneo said in English as he stood up. 'You move, I shoot.'

Keeping his pistol aimed in the man's direction, Tsuneo walked slowly toward the gravestone where he was hiding. The man didn't move. He was sitting on the ground behind the stone with his back to Tsuneo. His right leg was extended, and he was clutching his thigh with both hands. It was clear even from behind that he was enduring great pain.

'What happened? Are you hurt?'

Leaning back and peering over his shoulder at Tsuneo, the young man gave voice to the pain he had been holding in.

'Mr Kasama!' Sakuma was calling him from the apartment.

'It's okay,' Tsuneo shouted back. 'I'll bring him over.'

And then, all of a sudden, it happened. A bolt from the blue. A feeling totally unrelated to the situation he was in. Tsuneo opened his mouth slightly, just barely managing to keep from being forced to his knees by the tremendous force of what he was experiencing. He had no idea what was happening.

He heard Sakuma call back spiritedly, way off in the distance: 'Ai shii!' Tsuneo was the only one caught up in this sudden gust of feeling. He didn't even have the presence of mind to feel bewildered.

The young man was saying something. Please let me go, he was saying. If I'm deported now, all the money I spent to get to Japan and the twelve months I've been working – it will all have been for nothing.

Tsuneo was in no condition to reply. I can't let my grip weaken, I can't drop the gun – that's all he was thinking. The bastard. Acting like he doesn't know what's happening . . . he must have done something to me. Tsuneo tried to get a good look at the young man's face, but he couldn't make his eyes focus. He was aware that the graveyard around them was utterly still. He knew he was the only one caught up in this maelstrom.

The young man was thanking him. Tsuneo had lowered the pistol, it dangled from his hand. The man had misunderstood – that's why he was thanking me. What the hell is this guy thinking! The man started moving away, dragging his foot. Stop! The law is the law! An immigration officer can't come out on a raid and let just one guy in a whole group get away!

But Tsuneo was still in the grip of a violent sense of pleasure; it wouldn't let go. It had burst upon him like a sudden blast of wind, making the blood run hot in every vessel in his body, trying to rob him of his strength. What's happening? Tsuneo gave in, bent to his knees. Why do I feel so aroused? It was as if, all of a sudden, he had been embraced by a naked woman with beautiful fair skin. And yet, even if he had been embraced like that – this was a graveyard, early in the morning, in March. Why the hell would he start feeling this way right in the middle of his work, when he was so tense? It was a storm that broke out of the blue. A raging, sweet storm, too powerful to resist . . . and yet he ought to have been just about as far away from sexual desire as possible. He hadn't been looking for anything like that, not at all. All at once, the lower half of his body was overcome by a sensation like the one that hits the instant before ejaculation, and as he involuntarily jerked his torso back and tried to get control of himself, an overwhelming sense of warmth and sweetness coursed through his entire body. His consciousness of everything around him was forcefully wrenched away. Tsuneo resisted. He struggled to keep from dropping his pistol. And he didn't. It was all he could do to hold on. The young man fled. Dragging his foot as he ran. But there was no way Tsuneo could have pursued him. Why can't I follow? Did he hit me? Did he have a weapon? Which one of us has the hurt leg? How am I supposed to explain this? Who'd believe a ridiculous story about a feeling like this?

His hands were on the ground. He crouched there like a dog.

He heard panting. It was his own.

The earth felt cold. The storm was passing. There was a wet spot on his pants. That bastard. What did he do to me? With nowhere else to look for an explanation, he turned his gaze in the direction of the temple where the foreigner had gone. He felt so humiliated he couldn't even move. He would rather have been hit. But no, he had gotten down on his knees in front of a suspect he should have captured and surrendered himself to a wave of lust.

'Mr Kasama!' Sakuma was calling him from the road.

He had to do something. He had never screwed up like this before.

'Mr Kasama!' called Sakuma again.

'Yeah?' Tsuneo tried to sound in control.

'Where are you?'

'Over here.' There was no helping it. He picked himself up, exposing himself to the eyes of his inferiors. 'The bastard kicked my feet out from under me. He got away.' And just as the foreign youth had done, he pressed his hands against his right thigh and bit his lip.

2

When they returned to the office, Tsuneo reported the blunder he had made to Honda, the Chief Security Officer.

In the minibus on the way back, Miyazaki had kept insisting, a bit too persistently, that there was no need to report it. 'C'mon, there won't be any problem as long as the three of us keep our mouths shut. I mean, we set out to bring in six guys and we're coming back with seven, right?'

But Tsuneo didn't want to owe Miyazaki for something like this.

Honda just said, 'What're you gonna do, huh?' Then, 'You'll be able to identify him when you investigate those guys you brought in. Just be glad you weren't seriously injured.'

There were only about six hundred and fifty officers, people like Tsuneo, in all the Immigration offices around the country.

Their efforts led to the discovery every year of approximately fourteen to fifteen thousand men and women living in Japan in violation of immigration laws. The estimated total number of illegal immigrants was, however, somewhere between sixty and seventy thousand. Because of this officers sometimes found themselves overcome by a feeling of helplessness. They had to try and bring in as many people as possible, each one was important, otherwise their work would hardly make a dent in those vast numbers. The loss of this young man was particularly jarring to Tsuneo, due in part to the fact that he had never made such a blunder before, but it goes without saying that there was more to it than that.

Tsuneo had experienced something bizarre. And he couldn't help suspecting it had something to do with that young man – that wide-eyed, Indian-looking foreigner. I mean, how could the guy have made that happen? Was it magic? I've never heard of magic like that, but I guess it's possible. When you work with people from foreign countries on a daily basis, you can't help being struck by the fact that no matter where they come from, everyone feels the same emotions. But on the other hand, it's not all that infrequently that you come face to face with 'the Other' – with people so different you don't have the slightest idea what to make of them.

Sometimes friendliness is interpreted as contempt, but you get used to situations like that, and you learn to cope. And there are tremendous differences from country to country in people's preferences regarding members of the opposite sex. Tsuneo had been so shocked he actually gasped when someone pointed out to him that a woman considered beautiful in one country might be classified as ugly in another. Still, it's not as if it didn't make sense to him once he had been told. Every so often, though, he found himself shaken by the realization that he didn't have the slightest clue what a particular foreigner was thinking or feeling.

Of course it was completely natural for men and women being taken in to hide their emotions from the officers taking them in, and Tsuneo had no intention of letting himself get swept up in a surge of exaggerated emotion over something like that. Somewhere along the way, though, he had come to believe in the existence of the Other – of people who possessed depths that were totally beyond him.

The world we Japanese are able to grasp intuitively is extraordinarily narrow; in fact, most of what goes on around the globe wouldn't make the slightest sense to us if we knew about it. Let's face it, I wouldn't even be able to empathize with most of the customs, sensibilities, beliefs, and forms of consciousness that exist out there. This understanding of reality lay somewhere in back of Tsuneo's mind. He wouldn't have been surprised to learn of the existence of even the most improbable sort of magic.

But what the hell is a person involved in immigration control supposed to do if something like that is starting to be used in Japan? It isn't just immigration control, either. That stuff could be used to commit all kinds of crimes. Police officers would have the same problem – there's no way they could fight off that storm. Tsuneo thought it unlikely that many people could manage to hold their ground in the face of such a powerfully sensuous attack.

That afternoon, Tsuneo called Emoto, who was an Assistant Security Officer at the Yokohama Branch Office. The Tokyo Immigration Bureau has one branch in Narita and one in Yokohama. Emoto had been appointed in 1982, at the same time as Tsuneo.

When Tsuneo asked if they could get together that night somewhere in Kawasaki, Emoto jumped to conclusions. 'Wow, that was fast!' he said. 'So you're already worrying about who you can get to be master of ceremonies at the wedding, huh?' Apparently he'd heard about Tsuneo's introduction to Shibata Yoshie.

'No, no, it has nothing to do with all that.'

'What do you mean, "all that"? Don't treat it so lightly, man, just 'cause you've got someone. I mean, isn't there someone out there for me? Anyone?'

Even if I tell him, Emoto won't believe me. And yet Tsuneo had the sense that, of all of his friends, Emoto would probably be the most receptive. The other guys he knew wouldn't even recognize the facts. Some of these men were so stiff and serious you could hardly believe it. Tsuneo was a dedicated worker himself, sure, but there were times when he had his doubts, times when he seriously wanted to chuck it all away. His friends knew about this side of him. If he told them the story, they would probably just chalk it up to his 'softness'. Or interpret it as a really bad excuse. Or maybe they would decide there was something wrong with him and start worrying, even though there was really nothing to worry about.

Or should I be worried? Maybe I should. After all, he couldn't guarantee that he wasn't having mental problems. The feeling that came over him had come from outside, though. He really didn't think it could have been happening inside him. Of course, if there *were* something wrong with him, there was no telling how he might perceive things, no matter what the facts were.

* * *

'So did he do anything?' asked Emoto.

'Of course – he was here illegally. That's why –'

'No, not that kind of thing. I mean like, *abracadabra* . . .' Emoto wove his hands back and forth over the table at the *yakitori* restaurant, as though he were casting some sort of spell. 'You know, that kind of thing.'

'No. He just kept thanking me. Thanking me, dragging his leg.'

'Did you have a lotta stuff piling up?' Emoto pointed down at the lower half of his body. 'You know what I mean . . .'

'I'm single, what do you expect? But I wasn't feeling like that at all.'

'And what happened?'

'What do you mean?'

'Did you go into the minibus like that, with your pants wet?'

'I rubbed dirt on them to cover the spot. I went to the bathroom in the temple and got rid of my underpants too.'

'You didn't flush them down the toilet!'

'Of course not! I pushed them down into this big wooden box where they collect the dried-up flowers from the graveyard.'

'I bet it was something in the graveyard. Maybe the cremated remains of some sex maniac are buried there, in one of the untended graves.'

'Yeah, maybe.'

'Hey, I'm just kidding! Don't nod like you think I'm serious!'

'I know, it's just that when you're trying to find an explanation for something as pathetic as this, everything that comes to mind seems like a joke.'

'Look, I think you should just forget it.'

'I can't.'

'No one's blaming you, right?'

'That doesn't mean I can just forget it.'

'Why not?'

'It's just so unbelievable. I mean, isn't it?'

'You were tired. Don't you get kind of weirdly excited when you're tired?'

'In a graveyard at the crack of dawn?'

'You can't deny it might happen.'

'I absolutely deny that it could happen. I was feeling tense! There's no way I'd get excited like that.'

'Whatever. Drink up. Don't worry about it.'

I don't know. Thinking back on it all now, I can certainly see that I was tense, but I wouldn't say I'd reached the limit. I knew the guy was injured. He couldn't resist. All I had to do was lead him away. The tension level was decreasing, not increasing. Just take the man away, he's not even resisting. Did I feel some sort of pleasure in the superiority of my position? I can't say for sure that I didn't. I can't say for sure that I've never felt a sense of pleasure when we suddenly burst into a house and lead off a person who's been staying there illegally. But I didn't have the presence of mind to feel that way this morning, and besides the sensation that came over me then wasn't like that – it was a different kind of pleasure. The feeling that was stirred up in me then was the desire for a woman. There was no sign of a woman there. All right, where does that leave me? The untended grave of a sex maniac? That's one thing I really can't rule out. There must have been plenty of women in those graves. It was all so extraordinary that any sort of explanation seemed possible.

'Wait and see what happens. We'll think about it seriously if it happens again.'

'I suppose you're right.'

'You're heading into a marriage, right? What are you doing wasting your stuff in a graveyard? Save the incredible, mind-blowing pleasure for me.'

'Sure.'

After that they talked about work. There aren't enough offi-cers. It's tough going everywhere these days – at both the branch offices, even out of the office.

Mind-blowing pleasure? You talk as if it were nothing at all! You think you'd still be saying that if it actually happened to you? These thoughts kept running through Tsuneo's mind until he realized that what he'd felt really had been a tempest of over-powering sensuousness. A gunshot of delicious sweetness so profound it was unlike anything he had ever experienced before. He'd been looking at it as something awful, but then pleasure of that magnitude isn't the sort of thing you encounter all that easily, even when you are looking for it. And there hadn't even been a woman involved.

Tsuneo parted from Emoto, who was heading back to his place in Kashimada on the Nanbu line, at Kawasaki Station. As he made his way to the government-run apartment building where he lived, near K. Station on the Sōbu line, Tsuneo sensed that a part of him, deep down in his heart, yearned to be buffeted once again by that storm. Not, of course, on the job. If it was going to happen, let it be on some night when he was all alone. He would gladly surrender his body to the feel-ing then, for as long as it lasted. Who in their right mind would resist?

That rapture. 'Let it come, let it come, the time we've all been dreaming of!' was how Rimbaud put it. Yes, that's just how it felt. As he began recalling once more the bliss he had felt that morning, a closed door swung open in his mind and memories of his time in Portland came gushing at him like a wave. He tried to stand up straighter. He put the lid back on his memories, turned the key in the door. An officer in the Immigration

Bureau has to maintain his dignity, even in private life. I have to remember to ask Director-General Saitō which of the various auspicious days in April will be convenient. Tsuneo needed to settle on a date to exchange wedding gifts with the Shibata family.

3

Following the meal at which they were introduced, Tsuneo had gone out with Shibata Yoshie four times, and they had then decided to get married. Yoshie waited until the day after his proposal to say yes. She was twenty-five years old – four years younger than him – and 163 centimeters tall, which made her twelve centimeters shorter than Tsuneo, who was 175. She wore heels, of course, so the difference wasn't all that noticeable when they were walking around town. She was a fair, plump young woman with rather heavy black eyebrows. She didn't like it that her gums showed when she laughed, so her left hand was constantly flitting around her mouth the first time they were introduced. She wasn't particularly beautiful, but she wasn't ugly, either.

Since Tsuneo started working at the Immigration Bureau, very few people had inquired about the possibility of arranging a marriage with him. He didn't have many opportunities to meet women, either. Besides, he was always busy. Once, he had started dating a woman only to have her disappear as soon as he told her he was an officer in the Ministry of Justice, Immigration Bureau. He had sat and listened as a colleague frustrated for the same reason tried to drink away his depression. Do you think policemen and tax inspectors have to go through this too? his friend had asked. I mean, what's so awful about this job? We're working for the good of the nation! It's true, though, Tsuneo thought, this job is pretty dry, and we're never actually able to go home at five-fifteen, when work is supposed to be over. Most days we have to stay in the office until eight or nine, and sometimes we have to be at work early in the morning to go out on raids and bring people in. But then, aren't all men's jobs like that, no matter where they work?

'Tsuneo is a very ordinary man,' Director-General Saitō had said when he and Yoshie were first introduced. Then he had started questioning him.

'So what was your hobby again?'

'I don't really have one.'

'Wrong answer. You probably go to the movies or something, right?'

'Sometimes. Maybe three or four –'

'Three or four movies a week? Sounds like a hobby to me!'

'Three or four times a year.'

'A year?'

'Exactly.'

'What do you mean, *exactly*? Trying to make things hard for the matchmaker, are you? Sheesh, what a joker.'

Finally Yoshie opened her mouth. 'What about music appreciation?'

'That's right!' chimed in Yoshie's mother, who had come along. 'That's what it said on the résumé we received,' she said, nodding, in her best special-occasion voice. 'I believe it mentioned records.'

'Good point,' Mr Saitō nodded vigorously. 'What kind of songs do you like?'

'Yashiro Aki and stuff. Ballads.'

'I'd hardly call that music appreciation.'

Tsuneo gave his head a hesitant scratch, then chuckled along with everyone else. He didn't own a single record or even a CD of Yashiro Aki's. He did have a few recordings of piano pieces by Mozart and Beethoven symphonies, but that was about it. He didn't listen to them much, either. He had only written the bit about music appreciation because he had nothing else to put in the hobby column. In the old days he'd listened to jazz and popular music all the time, so much so that it almost got to be too much, but now all that led him back to memories of Portland.

Right now it didn't matter in the slightest what sort of music he actually liked – it was a question of choosing to be the sort of man who claimed to like a certain type of song. They'd think he was slimy if he mentioned Mozart. And he knew practically nothing about recent trends in rock. He wasn't sure how Yoshie would react when he said he liked Yashiro Aki, but he had the idea it might at least make him seem like an easygoing, trouble-free sort of guy.

'I like . . .' Once more, Yoshie opened her mouth. She leaned over toward her mother and murmured, 'Mori Shin'ichi.' It was as if she were confessing a secret.

'Now that's real music, if you ask me!' Mr Saitō said, and burst out laughing.

The second time Tsuneo and Yoshie met, it was just the two of them. Yoshie talked about how wildly different credit union employees are from what they seem.

'Everyone acts so cute and girly at the window that customers actually tell clerks, Gee, it'd be so great if I could have a nice girl like you as my wife, you know, but boy are they wrong.

The moment we're in the lounge, it's all "that old hag" and "that shitty fart". There's this married woman who works part time, she stands in the lobby and directs customers to the appropriate counter, you know, and despite the fact that she's in her forties, these twenty-five or twenty-six-year-old girls have the nerve to shout at her, 'Do some work instead of just standing there!' and so on.

'And of course the men who work in the bank have been trained to regard people differently depending on how much money they've got. They think nothing at all of making a customer who's come to close an account wait for more than thirty minutes, but say some young teller lands a hundred-million-yen account, bam, just like that, well, all of a sudden even the manager himself talks to him politely.'

The way she told it, Yoshie was just doing her best to live an 'ordinary' life there, in the midst of everything she'd described. They met a third time, then a fourth, and after that Tsuneo began to sense a certain something in the air that suggested the time had come to make up his mind, and let Mr Saitō know what he thought of Yoshie.

It was all very peculiar. He was struck anew by the strangeness of this process: to think that so many people were choosing their partners, people with whom they'd pass the entire second half of their lives, in the course of just one or two months. In the end, he thought, I guess we humans don't really take our lives all that seriously.

They went to see a movie in Yūrakuchō, then took a walk in Hibiya Park. The sun had just set, and there was a slight chill in the air. There was hardly anyone around.

She might be kind of conventional, but she wouldn't be all

that bad a person to settle down with, to try to build a peaceful home. That was how he saw things.

'I don't want to make things difficult for you by dragging this out,' Tsuneo said by way of an introduction. 'As far as I'm concerned, I'd like to carry this discussion to the next stage. I'd be very happy if you would consent to marry me.'

'I . . .' said Yoshie. 'I mean, it's okay with me, but I think my parents should be, well, you know –'

'Oh, sure, absolutely! Talk it over with them first, then let me know your answer. There's no rush. I'll be waiting, though, and hoping.'

'All right.'

They walked along in silence for a little, then Yoshie moved her body closer to his. Tsuneo put his arm around her shoulder. On a narrow path that few people take, close to the Sakurada Gate of the old Edo Castle, he tried to kiss her, but all of a sudden she gave a little titter and pulled her face back. Tsuneo was shocked at how intensely flirtatious that burst of laughter had sounded.

'Sorry,' said Yoshie. Her tone sounded just like how he imagined it would at her window at the credit union. 'You don't smoke, do you, Mr Kasama? I smoke, you know, so it occurred to me that my breath might taste bad.'

'It doesn't bother me. I used to smoke too.'

'And you managed to quit? Wow.'

Then they kissed. Yoshie's breath reeked. Until then, Tsuneo had never even noticed that she smoked. There were bound to be all kinds of other things he didn't know about her. She pushed her tongue into his mouth.

For a moment, Tsuneo found himself remembering the

stories Yoshie had told him about what went on behind the scenes at the credit union. She had talked as if she were simply an observer, but who knew, maybe she was in there bad-mouthing 'the old hags' with the rest of them. She might go into the lounge for a smoke and bawl out the married part-timer. That didn't necessarily mean she was a bad or mean person, he thought. That's just how people are. Clearly there's no such thing as a person who's 'ordinary' and 'pleasant' and that's all there is to her. We're talking real flesh and blood here. These are modern times we're living in. Who cares if she smokes, if she's had a certain amount of experience with men, if there's a part of her that's not all that nice, a part of her that can be crude? That's how it goes. Even me, I'm no different. I guess everyone is like that. Ultimately it doesn't really matter who you end up with, things are bound to turn out the same.

'I'll need to discuss things with your father.'

'That's true.'

As they started walking, Yoshie's knees suddenly buckled, causing her to stagger. Tsuneo supported her with his arm, which was linked with hers.

'I feel so embarrassed,' she said, pressing her forehead into his shoulder.

Hmm. Maybe she's actually kind of sensitive, Tsuneo thought. It could be that the unselfconscious, obviously flirta-tious tone she'd used earlier and the fact that she'd used her tongue the very first time they kissed were just signs of inexperi- ence. If she were as wily as he had been thinking, she should be able to do a better job of playing the role of well-bred daughter. I guess she's a good person after all, Tsuneo thought, and put more strength into the arm he had wrapped around her shoulder. A sense of desire welled up inside him.

That was all that happened. He didn't suggest that they go to a hotel or anything. Yoshie probably would have gone along with him if he had. Something in the way she leaned up against him made that clear. But he didn't want to behave in that way.

Seven years had passed since Tsuneo left Portland, but the yearning he felt to be normal hadn't faded. He wanted to keep himself clean until he was married. This was a decision Tsuneo had made entirely on his own, of course, and for his own reasons; Yoshie might well think it absurdly arrogant.

Tsuneo went as far as Ginza Yonchōme with Yoshie, who would be heading back to Yōga on the Shintamagawa line. He had the feeling, when she turned and looked back at him after passing through the gate into the station, that he saw disappointment on her face. No, that's not true. He didn't notice anything at the time; it was only later, thinking back on the scene, that it came to seem that way.

Could it have been Yoshie? Is it conceivable that the sensations that raged through me like a storm this morning were, in fact, the secret desires she feels?

The night deepened, but still Tsuneo was unable to sleep. He lay there in his small bachelor's room in the company dorm with the lights on, staring at the ceiling.

The news that Yoshie had accepted Tsuneo's proposal was passed on to Director-General Saitō by her mother. Five days later, on the evening of the following Sunday, Tsuneo made a trip to the family's house to pay his respects to her parents. He explained that after his mother's death his father had remarried and moved to Tsu, in Mie prefecture, so it would be a

little while before he could come up to Tokyo. They had dinner with Yoshie's parents, her sister, and her brother; it was
past nine when Tsuneo took his leave. Yoshie saw him to the
station in Yōga, but of course there was no question of their
kissing there, so they just shook hands and said goodbye. It
would have been nice to go out on a date sometime soon, but
Tsuneo was busy with work.

At any rate, Tsuneo found it difficult to believe that Yoshie
was feeling the sort of desire he had been imagining. It hardly
seemed likely that she would harbor such strong emotions for a
man she had met through a matchmaker.

So was it just me, then? I've had to keep a lot of things suppressed these days, in this life I'm living. Could it be that I'm
under too much pressure, that what happened to me then was a
cry for help from some region in my own subconscious?

But no matter how many times he called the memory up, he
never had the sense that that's what it had been – a cry from
within. No, it seemed like a surprise attack launched by someone else, some unknown Other.

The dorm Tsuneo lived in was at the second intersection of
a narrow, one-way road that ran parallel to a national highway, and late at night the roar of trucks passing on the main
road was clearly audible. He was listening to that sound now.

It was past two. Suddenly a breath of cold air brushed across
his skin; it was as if something were moving closer to him,
approaching his spine. His body sensed it even before he was
conscious of it, and reacted with a shudder.

Something is . . . but where is it coming from . . . ? A sense
of unease welled up inside him, and without even thinking
what he was doing he found himself glancing around the

room. There was nothing there. Just this inexplicable feeling that something big was about to happen, taking hold of him . . . he tried to sit up. But he couldn't move, it was as though a spell had been put on him. It was a dream. He was dreaming, that's what it was. No, that wasn't it. This was no dream. His eyes were wide open. Just then he felt a gust of icy wind coming from the far side of the night, zooming at him like an arrow, drawing closer and closer as he watched – the sense of its imminence shuddered over him. It's coming, it's coming, *it's coming!* And yet he had no idea what it was. All he knew was this sense churning within him that something was coming toward him and there was no way he could escape it – a feeling so powerful it almost made him lose control. The cold wind that had seemed to him at first like an arrow kept growing as it approached, widening, becoming ever larger, swelling until it towered over him like a giant wave – and now as it prepared to strike him he had the sense that it was coming apart, falling to pieces. A wave breaking. Breaking over him. What is it? It was impossible to resist. It breaks. Before Tsuneo even realizes the wave is breaking, he has already been sucked inside, it's toying with him, he's unable even to cry out, struggles to find something to grab onto, flails about wildly.

But even as he struggled, he remained conscious. Conscious that his body was still lying peacefully in bed. That his small room wasn't being attacked by anything, nothing was moving, not even a speck of dust; the single overhead light was casting its glow across the ceiling, and nothing at all had happened.

There's something wrong with me. The thing is, I know that there's something wrong. My head is clear. I keep thinking that everything is okay because my head is clear . . . and yet he was still tossing in the waves. He fought with all his might to keep from being dragged away. He opened his eyes wide, opened his mouth, tried to remain conscious.

And then, suddenly, the wave passed.

It rushed back into the distance from which it had come. He watched it go. Everything he had felt was a fiction. Because nothing had really happened.

I'm okay now. I've made it through okay. The wave kept drawing back into the distance. He was staring at the ceiling with his eyes opened wide, and yet it seemed to him that he could actually see the wave receding, retreating into the darkness of the sky. Like a giant bolt of white cloth being rolled up, it slid away before his eyes into the distance.

And then a sense of grief for the wave welled up inside him. But why should he lament its passing? Why feel regret for a wave that had played with him as this one had, treating him like a toy?

He struggled to resist this feeling, almost giving voice to his opposition, attempting to clear his mind.

It wasn't the wave. No, it wasn't the wave he was sorry to see go. He could tell it wasn't that. But he couldn't imagine what else this feeling could be for. His heart was brimming with something akin to sadness, though. That much was clear.

And now, from the depths of his sadness, a terrible sense of lack came gushing up to the surface, writhing and gasping. The realization that something had happened that could never be undone cut into him like a knife.

Tears spilled from his eyes, though he couldn't have said why. Before he knew it, his whole body was racked with sobs.

This sadness isn't mine, he thought. Sorrow this deep and

heavy can't be mine. There was a time when I should have felt this, but back then I never felt as sad as I could have.

Tsuneo wailed.

And then this sadness retreated into the distance, as if it were abandoning him. Wait, stop! What's going on? It's that guy, from this morning. What are you trying to do to me? Stop! I'm not going to let you do this! I refuse to let you work your magic on me, entering me and playing around with me like this!

He knew he was staring at the ceiling, but at the same time he was peering up into a dark and distant sky. The profound sadness he'd felt was flying off into that sky, its cape flapping wildly behind it. It grew smaller and smaller, then vanished into the darkness.

Peering into the void, he saw lightning flicker through the distant clouds, a dull flash unaccompanied by any sound, as if the lightning were breathing.

'*Who are you?*'

Huh? He seemed to have heard a voice coming from the place where he'd seen the lightning. A few words, that was all. And it had been very far away. But it sounded as though it were calling him. A quiet voice, practically a whisper. This is ridiculous. How could I possibly hear a voice that far away if it's just a whisper?

Maybe I didn't exactly *hear* it, though. Maybe I just felt it.

'*Who are you?*'

He tried to call the words back, to hear what kind of voice it was, but the moment he tried it slipped away; it seemed to him that it could have been any sort of voice at all. A child's voice, a young girl's, a woman's.

'*Who are you?*'

Only the meaning lingered on in Tsuneo's heart.

What does that mean? Who are you? Are you asking who *I* am? You must be kidding. I'm the one who should be asking you who *you* are. You come here of your own volition and start asking me who *I* am? I don't think so.

Still, he felt no antagonism toward the voice. The sadness that had cut through him earlier had been so deep that it seemed cruel to hate the person to whom, for all he knew, that emotion might well belong.

Hold on a second . . . hold on! What about that storm of sensual feeling that hit me this morning? Could that feeling have belonged to whoever was just speaking to me now too? If so, this person is a real devil. '*Who are you?*' As if I'd tell you. I'm not dumb enough to answer the devil.

The devil? What am I talking about? I've got to calm down. I can't let myself get sucked into this. When you get right down to it, neither of these things, what happened this morning and what happened just now, has anything to do with external reality. I shouldn't be taking a hallucination like this seriously. This kind of thing sends people to the shrink.

There's something wrong with me. I have to admit that. I've been talking big, but ultimately I just couldn't deal with it all. It's funny, though, I didn't really feel like I was in that bad a state. I never felt sick or anything. I suppose that's how it is with mental illness. I don't know, though – it really did feel as if that storm this morning, and the wave tonight, both came from outside.

4

'The part about what happened in the morning is pretty incredible, isn't it?' said the forty-something psychiatrist, being careful not to let his expression betray any sign of emotion. 'I'd say that's a very unusual experience.'

'Yes.'

'The part about that night makes sense. People suffering from depression often start feeling sad for no obvious reason; it's one of the symptoms. There are some good medications for that.'

'Oh.'

'What do you think about all this? About why you had these hallucinations?'

'I figured I was just exhausted.'

'How does this sound to you? That young Bangladeshi guy got away from you; you hated having to admit that, so you made up a story to explain it.'

'Absolutely not!'

'Sorry. Making people angry is one of our techniques. Some people start talking when you do that.'

'I thought I was already talking.'

'You graduated from high school, failed your university entrance exams twice.'

'Yes.'

'You went to America the winter of the second year after high school.'

'Yes.'

'Spent two years on the west coast, returned to Japan, and took one of the civil service exams open to high-school graduates.'

'That's right.'

'I got the sense you didn't want to talk about your time in America.'

'It's not that. I just didn't think it was relevant. It was a long time ago.'

Tsuneo lowered his gaze. He started to wonder if it might help to talk about what had happened there. But then, ever so casually, the psychiatrist glanced up at the clock on the wall.

'I'll write you a prescription for a mild antidepressant. I have a hunch that'll be enough, but if you'd like I can introduce you to a psychoanalyst I work with. You'd go to weekly sessions with him, and if those sessions indicated that further treatment is necessary we'd think about that then. How does that sound?'

Maybe I should just be happy that the psychiatrist treated me as well as he did, considering that I came without a referral. The waiting room was crowded. Tsuneo said thank you, picked up the medication at the attached pharmacy, and went back to the office. He told people it had taken an unexpectedly long time for him to question people about a factory in Nerima ward. That was the only way he could get to the psychiatrist without anyone knowing.

He was still in the office finishing up work when Yoshie called, a little past eight. She used her given name, not her family name, when she said hello. She hadn't done that before.

'I heard from Mr Saitō that the engagement ceremony has been scheduled for the twenty-ninth. That's a national holiday, isn't it?'

'That was the only day the Director-General could make it.'

'Oh, I see.' After that, Yoshie's voice changed. 'Are you still working?' she asked, in a tone that suggested pouting, upturned eyes.

'Yeah. It's just impossible for me to get out any earlier.'

'I'll have to prepare myself, huh? Tell myself you're going to be late every night, even after we're married . . .'

'I'm afraid this is one thing that isn't likely to change.'

'That's okay. I'm going to keep working too – who knows, maybe some nights I'll come home even later than you.'

'Listen, I'll call you.'

'Huh?'

'I mean . . . not now, you know.'

'Oh, I see. People will tease you, right?'

'Yeah.'

Yoshie laughed, tickled. 'Okay!' she said with a chuckle. 'Bye!'

'Yes . . . goodbye.'

'Hmm! That sounded pretty cold!'

'Sorry.'

'Anyway, I was *hoping* we might have a date this weekend? Can we?'

'Okay.'

'I can see you're pretty shy, huh.'

'No, no – I don't think that's true.'

After he hung up, Tsuneo was startled to find himself feeling a little sentimental. He had never seen this girlish side of Yoshie before.

So far, each time the two of them had met, some part of them was always busy evaluating the other. There had been a certain amount of tension between them, too. They hadn't been entirely at ease with each other, even when they went to the station together in Yōga after things were settled. But when they were talking on the phone just now, Yoshie had radiated something like the sweetness and joy one expects from a young woman talking with her fiancé. Somehow our engagement doesn't seem entirely real, not to me. Yoshie sure got used to it quickly, though. Seems she's feeling readier by the minute. I guess that's just the way it is, huh?

Suddenly Tsuneo felt a smile coming to his lips. He scrunched up his eyebrows and gave a little cough to try to hide it.

It seemed so strange that only a month or so after they had first met, this woman was prepared to spend the rest of her life with him.

He noticed, though, that for the first time he himself was feeling a placid sort of happiness at having found a person like her. Whatever his motives, this was the life he had chosen. And what the hell is a man going to do if he isn't happy with the life he's chosen for himself? he thought. I'm not going to have hallucinations any more. What was I thinking? I don't need antidepressants! I never believed I was that run down mentally. It was a mistake to go and see that psychiatrist. I don't know why I had those hallucinations, but I know it doesn't have anything to do with my mind. It must have been some kind of spell after all, something that guy put on me as a last resort. But if that's the case, what need was there to have me hallucinate again that night, after he'd already got away? Was it just to harass me? Would a guy in his position have the time to sit around doing stuff like that?

'*Who are you?*'

Whatever. Forget it. Just forget the stupid voice.

'*Who are you?*'

Purge it from your memory. Why should you let it get to you?

'*Tell me, who are you?*'

Tsuneo gave a start. The hand he was using to write out his report stopped moving. There were still four or five people around him.

There was one female officer, but he knew it wasn't her. Because the fact of the matter was that he hadn't even really *heard* the voice. He had *felt* the words.

And the words came again.

'*Tell me, who are you?*'

Don't do this, please. Why are you talking to me? And who *are* you, anyway? I'm about to get married. I don't have time to hallucinate. Leave me alone. Go away.

He couldn't say any of this out loud. He gave his head an unobtrusive shake, trying to force himself to concentrate on his report. The voice didn't speak again.

5

Two days later, Emoto from the Yokohama Branch Office called him at work.

'So has anything happened since then?'

'Not really.'

'What you mean, not *really*?'

This wasn't something to discuss at work.

'Nothing's happened.'

'All right, it has to be that guy then. He must have cast a spell or something. There's no telling what sort of powers foreigners might have at their disposal. I mean, in India there are guys who can levitate, right? Let them into the country and you have to deal with that kind of thing, too. You have to let people live these lives that are totally different, you know – unfathomable. And what I'm saying is, are we really ready for that?'

'What are you talking about?'

'Oh, you know. Those people are at it again. Bastards are out there in front of the detention facility, saying things that make us sound like demons. How can you be so cruel, arresting them and chasing them out like that! The usual.'

'Don't let it get to you.'

'I'm not.'

Tsuneo often found himself thinking how much better

he'd feel if the foreigners they brought in tried to resist or used all kinds of devious tricks or were very strong. Hardly anyone they detained offered any resistance, and these people worked so hard, and even now that they'd made it to Japan they were barely managing to live at a subsistence level. How could anyone see that and not feel for them? Tsuneo constantly had to keep his emotions in check. True, it would be a disaster if they just threw open the gates at the borders, got rid of all restrictions entirely. And no doubt those shallow humanists would be the very first to fall speechless in the face of what would follow. Yes, Tsuneo was perfectly aware of all that. And to a certain extent, he did feel a sense of mission. It was just that he found it impossible to love his work. Six years earlier, during the one period in his life when he felt least inclined to have anything to do with foreigners, he had got this job. Among all the national civil service exams open to high-school graduates, this was the only one that included English. He took the job because he had no choice. It was as though something or someone had ordered him to take it. He wanted to punish himself.

'What happened to the guy who got away?' asked Emoto.

'No one's talking. We don't even know his name.'

'I'd like to meet him if you end up bringing him in.'

'Why?'

'I want to ask him if I can be his disciple.'

Emoto chuckled, then hung up.

As long as nothing else happened, as long as life just went on as usual, he could forget all about that day. He didn't need to come to any conclusion as to whether it had been a spell cast on him by that guy, a trick played on him by a ghost in an untended grave, or a result of his own weakness. He didn't like leaving things in this uncertain state, but then on the other hand he didn't think it would do him any good to keep worrying either. '*Tell me, who are you?*' Make the mistake of answering a question like that and you could well end up getting drawn into that other world.

That other world? What the hell am I talking about?

That evening, a group of three officers under the command of the security officer who had scouted out the place the previous day went into an apartment in Ōkubo, Shinjuku ward. They detained five Filipino women, jailing them in the Ōtemachi Office, in accordance with the warrant. They would have to write up the report and hand the suspects and all the evidence over to the immigration inspection officers within forty-eight hours.

These inspectors were the ones who would judge the suspects and issue the orders for their deportation. It was them, the upper ranks. Becoming an inspector is one of the goals on which immigration officers set their sights. It should be noted in passing that once the inspectors issued their orders, the women would have to be transported under escort to the Yokohama Immigration Center.

It took until after midnight just to write up the report. By the time Tsuneo made up his mind not to go home and went up to the rest station on the third floor, it was already one o'clock.

Tsuneo secretly felt afraid to go back and sleep in his own room at the dorm. The past two nights, he had been unable to shake off the feeling that he needed to be prepared in case he was attacked by another hallucination, and so he had slept very poorly. He was exhausted. He wanted to go straight to sleep here in this room, in which three or four other men were already sleeping. He drank a prepackaged cup of sake and lay down. Even so, a part of him was waiting. You want to mess with me? Just try. I'm not just going to lie here and let you fool with me this time, he thought. Without even realizing it, he had started listening intently. He had no idea when he fell asleep. Nothing happened.

* * *

Tsuneo felt a slight sense of disappointment when he started work the next morning. Three days had passed without any untoward occurrences, and now somehow he felt as if something was missing. Part of him was waiting for that storm, the wave, the whispering to return. Looking back, it occurred to him that during the hallucinations he had actually been in a state of ecstasy. He had been forced to submit without any possibility of resistance, he had been mercilessly toyed with, and as a result he had felt both fear and humiliation; at the same time, though, something in the experience attracted him. He had felt something then that was impossible for him to feel in his daily life.

'Tell me, who are you?'

That voice wasn't speaking inside him, that was clear. At the time, it felt as if someone were talking to him, trying to strike up a conversation – that's what it was closest to. So maybe that was really what had happened? The owner of the voice started talking to him, but without knowing who he was?

Tsuneo gave a wry grin. I'm letting myself get too involved in this again.

But unlike yesterday, he didn't immediately try to draw back, to put an end to what was happening. Never in his life had he experienced sexual pleasure as overwhelming as the ecstasy that had come over him in the graveyard that morning. He had felt at peace somehow, even as he was being swept up by that enormous wave, his arms and legs flailing about as though he were nothing but a doll.

'*Tell me, who are you?*'

Not a good idea to answer that question. The fact that the voice's owner didn't know who Tsuneo was put a very strong card in his hand. She had enough power to make him have some pretty incredible hallucinations. He certainly shouldn't give her any more advantages. I'm an ordinary twenty-nine-year-old man. I don't think I can say any more than that.

'*You're twenty-nine?*'

'That's right. Twenty-nine and single.'

'*How wonderful! We're talking, you and I.*'

Tsuneo slammed down the binder holding the reports with a bang, causing a few people to look up. 'Hey, Sakuma!' he shouted, as if to beat back their gazes. 'Could you give me a hand here? You took the call from that Japanese language school in Tabata, right? From the staff member?' He was heading toward the hall as he spoke.

'Yeah. That call just reeked of revenge, though. It was a snitch.'

'I don't care what it reeked of.' Tsuneo was walking down the hall, toward the stairs. 'The motive isn't important.'

'Is this going to take time?'

It wouldn't take any time at all. He didn't need Sakuma's help. He suppressed the shock he was feeling.

They were talking. He was still talking to that voice.

'*How wonderful. We're talking, you and I.*'

'Forget it,' said Tsuneo, stopping suddenly in the stairway. Then, looking back over his shoulder, 'It's okay. I'll take care of it myself.'

'No, no – I can do it. What do you want me to do?' Sakuma was just starting down the stairs.

'No, never mind. I'll take care of it. Thanks.' He reached the second floor.

'Are you upset with me or something?' Sakuma chased after him, looking like he didn't know what to do.

'I'll take care of it, forget it.'

'Tsuneo, don't sulk like that!'

Tsuneo went down to the first floor without stopping, strode past the foreigners waiting for the elevator, and walked out the front door. The Immigration Bureau counter that dealt with foreign residents was located on the second floor. The first and second floors of the building were always packed with foreigners who came to apply for extensions of their residency period or to change their visa status. The benches filled up immediately, and people overflowed into the halls.

Some people thought the Immigration Bureau did this intentionally. They said the officials were worried that the number of applicants would increase if they made the environment at the counter more pleasant. It was kind of a low way of doing things, though. If they wanted people to have a good impression of Japan, they ought to increase the number of staff members and make the area bigger. Every time he saw this crowd, he wondered where all the money was that Japan was supposed to have. The majority of the foreigners who come to that counter to file applications must leave it disliking Japan. Forcing himself to focus on these thoughts, Tsuneo walked into the forest of buildings.

6

'*Good evening,*' the woman said.

There was no one in the room. Tsuneo had just come home. He had walked through the door, switched on the light, and was standing there with his shoes on, leaning his back against the closed door. It was a little after ten-thirty.

The woman's voice spoke.

'*Good evening.*'

He was unsure whether or not he ought to reply.

He'd been thinking about it on the way home. Wondering whether, once he was back in his room, all alone, the woman would speak to him again. The closer he got to his dorm the stronger his premonition became, so that when he did actually hear the woman's voice in his head, he couldn't be sure whether it was a real woman's voice or an imaginary one created by his own heightened sense of anticipation.

'*You hear me, right?*' said the woman. '*You hear my voice?*'

'Yeah.' Tsuneo spoke aloud, as if testing his ability to speak.

'*Good evening!*' the woman's voice leapt.

Is it possible I'm only hearing this voice because I want to? I mean, I'm on the verge of exchanging engagement gifts. Why would I want to hear another woman's voice at a time like this? I guess I might feel a desire like that in a casual sort of way, that's possible, but it hardly seems likely I'd feel such a strong desire for another woman's voice that I'd actually start to hear it, as vividly as if it were real.

'Let me ask you something,' Tsuneo said quietly to the empty room.

'*Okay.*'

'Do you really exist? Or are you just a figment of my imagination?'

'*I really exist.*'

Naturally, this response could be a figment of his imagination, too.

'Can you prove that?'

'*Wait.*'

Tsuneo didn't move. He tried to keep his mind as empty as possible. None of this would mean anything if he were just telling himself to wait, and then thinking up a response himself. Some form of proof was needed that clearly could only be attributed to a person other than himself.

'*Turn to face this way,*' said the woman's voice.

He gave a start. 'Which way?'

Is she here? In this room?

'Where are you?'

'*No, no. It's a haiku.*'

'A haiku?'

'*Yes, a haiku.*'

'A poem? That kind of haiku?'

'*Do you know that haiku? "Turn to face this way —"*'

'No, I don't.'

He didn't know anything about haiku.

'*Me neither. But I remember this one. Sometimes I like to say it to myself.*'

'"Turn to face this way –"?'
'*Yes. Try to say the rest.*'
'I couldn't even guess.'
'*It's by Bashō.*'
'It doesn't matter who wrote it, I don't know it.'
'*I can say the rest, so I'm not you.*'
That made sense.
'Let's hear it.'
'"*Mine as well, this loneliness.*"'
'And then?'
'*You don't remember it?*'
'I never knew it.'
'"*The end of autumn.*"'
'"Turn to face this way –"'
'*Yes.*'
'"Mine as well, this loneliness / the end of autumn."'
'*Yes.*'
'I've never heard that before.'
'*Okay, that's enough.*'
'Enough what?'
'*I get tired . . . wears me out.*'
Suddenly the tension that had hovered in the air around him was gone. Nothing but reality remained. That's how it felt.

Tsuneo slowly removed his shoes, stepped up into the room, dropped to his knees, and sat down.

Turn to face this way –
Mine as well, this loneliness
The end of autumn.

He had never heard a haiku like that before. He was sure of it. Which meant she existed. The woman existed. He had talked with the woman. In an odd way.

He realized for the first time how exhausted he was. He'd worked hard, so maybe it was that. Or maybe it was from talking with the woman. Or maybe it was both.

Tsuneo collapsed where he was and fell asleep. When he woke the next morning he realized he hadn't even turned out the light.

7

People can marry without being in love. Arranged marriages offer just about the best possible proof of this, so it would have been silly for Tsuneo to trouble himself about whether or not he was in love with Yoshie. Pressed to declare himself one way or the other, he would certainly have said he didn't love her.

Presumably there are cases where men and women actually do come to love each other deeply just over a month after their first meeting, but most arranged marriages aren't like this: the bride and groom manage to get through it all either by looking the other way and ignoring reality, or by hurriedly creating within themselves the illusion that they're in love.

Before the formal engagement ceremony took place, Tsuneo and Yoshie needed to choose an engagement ring together. They arranged to meet at a coffee shop in Shibuya one Sunday afternoon. It was there that he mentioned his budget.

He was planning, he said, to spend about three hundred thousand yen for both the engagement and the wedding rings, but since they were meant to last a long time, he was prepared, and even happy, to spend a hundred thousand more.

'I'd feel bad making you spend so much,' Yoshie said, looking so genuinely sorry that Tsuneo was taken by surprise.

'Don't worry,' said Tsuneo, feeling a burst of affection for

Yoshie. 'Strange as it may seem, I'm twenty-nine. I can manage that much.'

Yoshie had yet to explain, however, why it was she felt bad.

'I don't know how to say this.' She lowered her eyes.

'What?'

'You see, *I've* been . . .' Yoshie put particular emphasis on the *I've*. 'It's just, I've been at the credit union since high school, you know, so *I* have some . . .' Again, she put emphasis on the *I*.

'Look,' Tsuneo smiled, 'whatever it is, just say it.'

She paid only thirty thousand a month for her apartment, so she had some savings of her own. The engagement ring was something she'd treasure for her whole life, she said, so she was wondering if it would be okay with him if she added two hundred thousand of her own and selected something for about five hundred thousand.

'Of course,' she concluded, 'I'll just forget it if that makes you angry.'

'I'm not angry at all. How's this sound, then? We'll throw in your money and budget five hundred thousand just for the engagement ring. We'll use the additional hundred thousand I was prepared to spend for the wedding rings. Is that okay?'

'Okay.' She nodded, trying to look cute.

Since there was no real love between them, holding them together, they couldn't afford to treat the ring lightly. By investing money in things like this, they could gradually give weight to their marriage. Tsuneo could understand that feeling.

The credit union where Yoshie worked was in Sangenjaya; apparently they could get a twenty percent discount at a jewelry store there that had an account at the credit union. They went to the store, taking the Shintamagawa line. They bought a platinum ring with a 0.8 carat diamond. This meant the wedding rings would have to be platinum too, of course. They decided to select the design later.

'I don't want to rush through it all, you know, as if we're just taking care of business,' Yoshie said to the owner of the store, laughing.

Tsuneo stood with his back to her, listening, wondering whether something in his attitude had made Yoshie feel he was just 'rushing through it all'.

He had to prepare for the wedding in the intervals between work, that was true, and his work kept him very busy. There was just no escaping a certain sense of hurriedness, as if they were 'taking care of business'. When you got right down to it, this was all part of the process, and he would have preferred it if Yoshie hadn't tried to make everything so sentimental. Though of course he understood how she felt.

They went down to the platform to catch the subway back to Shibuya.

'I looked in a book and found one French restaurant and one Japanese restaurant that I think might be good. What do you feel like having?'

'You bought me such a gorgeous ring, I'll treat you.'

'That's okay. I mean, you paid for two-fifths of it.'

'Just forget about that. Don't mention it to my parents either, okay?'

'I wish I could have paid the whole five hundred thousand myself.'

'No, no. I was planning to add my bit, no matter what your budget was. The extra two hundred thousand lets me show off.'

'Oh.' It struck Tsuneo that she was being awfully frank, but there was a part of her that seemed to be brushing off her own frankness with a wry smile, so he didn't feel overly put off. She's very matter-of-fact, he thought. She took the trouble to find out about the store with the twenty percent discount, but she wants to show off when she can, and now here she is, steadily making her way through the preparations for her marriage to a guy she still isn't even able to love . . . Suddenly he felt a deep sense of pity for Yoshie. Though of course, I'm in the same position myself.

They went into the Japanese restaurant and were seated at a table in the corner. They ordered the 'Setonai Prix Fixe Menu', as recommended by the book.

They had sake. Yoshie could drink a lot. By the time they finished their fourth small bottle her voice had grown a little louder, but that was all.

She started telling him more about the people at the credit union. The one about how the acting branch manager, a man in his forties, kept trying to seduce the married part-timer with gifts intended for customers was pretty good. Yoshie was extremely observant where other people were concerned. Tsuneo thought she would make an easy-to-get-along-with, dependable wife.

'You know, darling, I think you and I might just get along,' said Yoshie suddenly, echoing his thoughts. 'I'm chatty, and you hardly talk at all.'

'That's true.'

When two people who hardly know each other start living together, he thought, all sorts of unexpected things are bound to crop up, but at least I'll be better off with Yoshie than with one of these weirdly dreamy women.

'Talk to me,' Yoshie said, skillfully pouring him more sake. 'Tell me about something that happened recently or something.'

'Something that happened recently . . .'

'Exactly. Something that happened recently.'

The first things that came to mind were the storm, the wave, and the voice, but he doubted Yoshie would accept a story like that. She'd probably just find him creepy. He had the feeling that this was one of her good points: the fact that she wouldn't for a moment believe such a 'ridiculous' story.

'Lately –' he began.

'Yes?'

'I've been hearing a voice.'

'A voice?'

'It says good evening. There's no one around, but I hear this voice saying good evening to me.'

'Where?'

'Here and there. *Good evening.*'

'Are you drunk?'

'Yeah, I get drunk suddenly. Before I know it I can't even walk.'

'I was wondering what the hell you were talking about.'

Tsuneo laughed and let it drop. She wouldn't believe him even if he really tried to tell her. And it wasn't only Yoshie. No one would believe a story like this. He wanted to tell someone about it, but not many people would really be able to accept it. He wouldn't be able to talk with Yoshie about this, even after they were married. He'd just have to let it sink into oblivion, along with the story of what had happened in Portland.

* * *

'Good evening!' Arriving back at his dorm at slightly past eleven, Tsuneo called into his room, as if it were just a joke. 'Good evening!'

He collapsed onto his bed and chuckled quietly to himself. I'd pretty much lose all the trust people put in me if I told them I've talked with a woman in this room when there was no one here. I have no choice but to keep this a secret.

'The thing is, why the hell would you choose me? I'm not the kind of guy who likes these far-fetched situations, that's not my thing, and it's not like there's anything particularly interesting about me.'

'*Then what is it like?*'

'What's what like?'

'*You . . .*'

Tsuneo fell silent. Without realizing it, he had started talking with the woman.

'Now that's a surprise.' He took a deep breath. 'You're asking me what kind of a guy I am? You're the one who started talking to me. You ought to know, right?'

'*I was wishing. Wishing I could talk like this, to someone.*'

'Well then, who chose me?'

'*I guess you're the only one who answered my call.*'

'First of all, I didn't answer anything. I didn't even know you were sending out these signals – I was just taken by surprise and before I knew it, everything was a mess. That's what happened. Listen, I just want to confirm something. That thing in the graveyard was you too, right? You did that to me?'

'*The graveyard?*'

'You don't know about the graveyard?'

'*I don't know anything. I have no idea where you are, what your face looks like, what your body is like. I'm just amazed that we're talking like this.'*

'How can I explain it? At first, it was really erotic.'

'What?'

'You don't remember? Erotic . . . I mean, like a man and a woman . . .'

Suddenly, something in the air changed. The tension dissipated. It was a subtle but unmistakable shift, as if a single sheet of some thin film that hung in the air around him had fallen away.

'She's gone.'

Yeah, she's gone. In his drunkenness, Tsuneo laughed. Was it you? That was you in the graveyard too, huh?

'Hey, hey, what's the big deal?' he said, just to see what would happen. 'Pretty impressive, if you ask me. Feel absolutely free to do it again.'

But there was no longer any response.

'You're concerned with appearances. You're one of these people who clam up when they don't like how things are going.' Tsuneo was still talking when he fell asleep.

* * *

The next morning, however, as he and Inspector Ōta were heading out to conduct an inspection of a factory in Adachi ward that printed Japanese fans, he was puzzled to find that he had a hard time remembering how the voice had sounded the previous night.

Despite the amount of time they'd spent talking, his memory seemed to be able to go either way. When he told himself her voice was high-pitched, that seemed right; but then on the other hand if he told himself it was rich and deep, that seemed right too. Ordinarily this wouldn't happen. Normally when you talk with someone, your ears retain a memory of the quality of her voice. So I can't have been talking to anyone, after all. But I *was* talking to someone, that much is obvious. There's no question we were talking – so maybe it was like electrical waves or something that conveyed the meaning, not the sound? Except that it hadn't been just the meaning.

The distinctive rhythm with which each word had been uttered, deliberately, one after another, as if they were being wrung from the speaker . . . it still lingered in his heart, like a sort of sweet aftertaste.

The actual words she used weren't all that strange, but they had a secretive quality unlike anything he could expect to hear anywhere else. Compared to her voice, Yoshie's sounded garishly real, even violent. When you're listening intently to the feeble, faltering babble of an infant, and then all at once the fluid speech of a middle-school girl talking somewhere imposes themselves on your attention, butting in from the side, the latter is bound to strike you as being very rough. None of this really has anything to do with Yoshie and what she's like. It's the other voice that's special. There was nothing faltering about it, not at all; he just had the sense that it took a totally different level of concentration for the woman to pronounce each individual word. That was obvious enough. He had no idea where she was, but presumably she was far enough away that it'd be physically impossible for her voice to reach him. And yet she radiated each word, and they all arrived.

'Did you not get enough sleep or something?' said Ōta. He didn't talk much himself, but he seemed unable to bear the silence any longer.

'No need to get angry. I was just thinking. What was the question?'

'I didn't ask anything. There was a puddle.'

'Oh no, I'm wet.'

His left shoe was soaking.

'You just noticed that now?'

The moment he let his mind wander, he found himself mesmerized by last night's voice. It was like a whirlpool, drawing him in.

'*I don't know anything. I have no idea where you are, what your face looks like, what your body is like.*'

It's wonderful. It's awesome. Without anyone else knowing, a woman tried to radiate her thoughts, pouring her whole heart into the effort, and her thoughts actually made it to someone. The thing is, why did *I* receive them? It would make sense if I were feeling the same urge. But it never even occurred to me to feel something like that. It never occurred to me? I can't really be sure of that. I have developed a tendency to suppress my feelings. Trying to jump in all of a sudden and plumb the depths of my own psyche isn't going to help. I still won't know for sure.

C'mon, of course you know! All you have to do is listen. The truth is, you wanted this. You put a lid on your feelings when you took this job, you selected a marriage partner without asking yourself how you feel about her. You're not giving your own feelings the slightest consideration, are you? You always think you can get through just about anything, because all you have to do is suppress it.

'Huh?' Tsuneo glanced over at Ōta.

'Should we go around and question people?'

'That might hurt the company's relations with its neighbors. We'd better start with our own observations.'

A call had come in about this factory from a man, apparently in the same business, who claimed it employed 'a significant number' of Pakistani workers; Tsuneo and Ōta were just starting their investigation. The two men climbed up onto the bank of the Arakawa river. It was a warm morning, and spring was in the air.

8

'*What kind of work do you do?*' asked the woman.

'You tell me first,' replied Tsuneo.

'*I can't say.*'

'Why not?'

'*Because I want to be a mystery woman.*'

'Well, I want to be a mystery man.'

'*I told you how tired this makes me.*'

'Yeah.'

'*Help me out.*'

'What should I do?'

'*Feel like you want to talk with me.*'

'I already feel that way.'

'*Feel it more.*'

'Okay, I'll try.'

'*Oh, that's nice. It's easier. I feel more relaxed.*'

'There's one thing I want to ask you.'

'*All right.*'

'How old are you?'

'*I wonder . . .*'

'Look, neither of us knows who the other is. You can tell me.'

'*Eighteen.*'

'You're lying.'

'Twenty-one.'

'It's hard to talk to you when I don't know how old you are.'

'Twenty-six.'

'That makes more sense.'

'*I'm twenty-six.*'

'Fine.'

'*All right then.*'

'What do you mean, all right then?'

'*Talk to me.*'

'I'd rather you talk to me. You wanted to talk, right?'

There was no response. He listened.

'Hello?'

'*Yes?*'

'It's like being on the phone.'

'*Yeah, that's true.*'

'I thought the line had gone dead.'

'*This is hard.*'

'What is?'

'*It's hard to know what to talk about if I'm going to remain a mystery woman.*'

'All right then, why don't you forget about that and just go ahead and tell it all to a man you don't know.'

'*Tell it all?*'

'Yeah.'

'*Maybe you're right.*'

'It's not often one can interact with someone like this. I won't use you.'

'*Use me?*'

'I mean, I won't take advantage of things you tell me to try to mess with you.'

'*That hadn't even occurred to me.*'

'That's all right, then.'

'*The ocean is lovely.*'

This was unexpected.

'The ocean?'

'*Yes. The ocean. There isn't a single boat as far as I can see. I love the ocean at this hour, as the day is breaking.*'

'As the day is breaking?'

'*I like the sound of the waves too. Something about the waves at night makes you hold your breath, wondering whether their pounding might not be drowning out some other sound. A sense of unease wells up in me, because I think the noise of the waves may be covering up the sound of someone coming up the stairs, opening the door . . . but even so, I still love the sound of the waves at dawn.*'

'But it's not dawn now.'

'*That's true. It's morning now.*'

Tsuneo didn't move.

Lying on his back in bed, he slowly opened his eyes.

'*Hello?*' said the woman.

A huge hand wraps itself around Tsuneo's stomach and steadily tightens its grip.

'*Hello?*'

He didn't even have to look at the clock, because it was obvious. It was just past eleven at night now. Of course it wasn't dawn. Of course it wasn't morning.

'Where are you?'

'*Where do you think I am?*'

'I know. Of course I know.'

'*Of course?*'

'You're no woman. I thought there was something strange about you right from the start. You don't have the *scent* of a real woman. I have to say, though, you sure go to great lengths to frighten a person. The time difference, huh? Talking about the time was your way of clueing me in. You're enjoying yourself, Eric, aren't you? Yeah, Eric – it's you all right. What are you trying to do, getting into my head like this, after all this time? Get out. What happened that day wasn't my fault. It was a misunderstanding between you and them. I'm not saying I didn't do anything. But you're the one who made me do what I did. You drove me to it.'

There was a sound. He knew what it was. It was someone knocking. Whoever it was sounded angry. Someone was annoyed. It was probably the guy next door, the guy from the Ministry of Agriculture, Forestry, and Fisheries. This was an official dormitory inhabited by civil servants, so there were all kinds of people here.

'Mr Kasama!'

Sure enough, it was the guy next door.

'Yes?'

He tried to make his voice sound as normal as possible.

'Is something the matter?'

'No, everything's fine.'

'Are you sure?'

'I'm sorry.'

'Do you have company?'

Man, this guy won't leave things alone. 'No, it's just me,' Tsuneo said in an especially cheerful voice, then ran to the door and suddenly flung it open. His thirty-four-year-old neighbor lost his balance as he tried to leap out of the way of the door, then let out a burst of laughter that sounded like a scream.

'I was practicing reading aloud, and I got carried away.'

'Your face is pale.' As if that were any of his business! 'You're all sweaty.'

'Yeah, I really got into it. Sorry. I'll keep quiet from now on.'

'I don't mind, it's just –'

Then leave!

Tsuneo slammed the door so forcefully it created a breeze.

Why, seven years later, am I still letting this bother me? This deep psyche stuff is too much. Who'd have guessed Eric would turn up like this, in this way?

Eric Roob. He had a weird last name. *Roob*. He told me he was born near Lake Michigan. He's been dead for ages. If this is his ghost, it ought to have appeared a lot earlier. For me to start being haunted by him now, after all this time . . . though I suppose it makes more sense to see this as an issue of my own, something in my own heart. If so, though, my unconscious sure goes to a lot of trouble – bringing Eric out like this, in the form of a woman's voice. And introducing this stuff about the time difference and all . . . It's true, right now it's morning in Portland. Can it be that all this time, deep down in my heart, I've been keeping track of things like that, like what time it is in Portland? I had no idea. I never realized I had this messed-up, twisted side to me.

Again he couldn't sleep. No sooner did he start to drift off than a sense of unease flickered through his body, rousing something deep within him. He'd be so happy if he could fall asleep right away and lie there as though he were dead, but it hardly seemed likely that he'd be able to now.

Shortly after three o'clock, Tsuneo was seized by the feeling that something or someone was stealthily sneaking up on him. He shuddered, sweat broke out all over his body, and, thinking it must be a dream, he began to sit up, trying as quickly as possible to make up his mind whether or not it was. But he couldn't move. He attempted to speak, to say, 'So this is what it means to be hogtied', but his voice had been stolen too. He opened his eyes wide, trying to calm himself.

'*Please, listen to me.*'

The voice was right at his ear.

'Eric!' he shouted, but without making a sound.

'*Who's Eric?*'

'Go away!'

'*I'm not Eric.*'

'Go away, whoever you are!'

He couldn't actually speak, but clearly the woman could hear what he was saying. But it wasn't a woman. It was Eric disguised as a woman.

'*I lied. I'm in Tokyo. That just came to me. I wanted to seem mysterious. I figured you'd get a shock if I said it was morning in the middle of the night, so I lied. I was the one who got the shock, though. I never expected anything like that to happen.*'

'Things like that don't just come to you.'

'*Yes, they do. I have an uncle in Fresno who sends me letters. I know if you add seven hours to the time in Japan and change day to night, that's the time in California. Every so often I start wondering, you know? Hmm, what time is it in America now?*'

'Yeah, whatever.'

'*Please believe me.*'

'Go away.'

'*I'm not Eric.*'

'All right, then what do you have to do with him?'

'*Nothing. I don't know anyone named Eric.*'

'Don't use that innocent tone of voice with me! You have to be pretty strong to hold down a grown man. Isn't that right? Let me go, you devil!'

'*I'm not a devil.*'

'Don't bother me again. I'll be a married man soon. I don't have time to fool around with you.'

'*You're getting married?*'

'Yeah, I'm getting married.'

'*You're lying . . .*'

'Lying? Why do you say that?'

'*No one happy enough to get married would be able to hear my voice.*'

'Well then, there must be some mistake. Turn in some other direction and grab hold of someone else, okay?'

'*You can't be getting married.*'

'We're having the engagement ceremony at one o'clock the day after tomorrow. I'm not making this up. I've bought all the gifts. And the engagement ring.'

'*But you're not serious about her.*'

'People don't do these things unless they're serious.'

'*That's not entirely true.*'

'I assure you I'm not the sort of guy to get married on a whim.'

He spoke these words forcefully, loudly – though of course it was all happening inside his head – and so roughly that it brought the conversation to an end.

The room was silent.

She wasn't gone, though. There was no change in the air around him. He tried to lift one of his hands, just to see what would happen, but it remained motionless, as though it were buried in cement. He saw how powerless he was.

'Listen.'

There was no response. The sense of terror he had been struggling to hold back slowly spread along his spine.

'Forgive me for speaking so roughly. There was a misunderstanding. You're not Eric. I see that now. I just went crazy, it had nothing to do with you. I want to apologize. I'm sorry. You're very powerful. There's no reason for you to talk with someone like me, I'm sure you can find someone much better, anyone you want. This has been an incredible, completely unexpected experience. Never in my wildest dreams did I imagine that humans have this kind of potential. I'm just amazed that it's possible for us to have a conversation like this. I know this is going to sound like out-and-out flattery, but there was something different about you that I found really attractive. To tell you the truth, after I started speaking with you I actually found it dull to talk to my fiancée. But I can't back out now. Please understand that. And once I'm married I won't be able to talk with you like this anymore, you know, so I'm going to have to stop doing this.'

Suddenly both of Tsuneo's arms gave a tremendous jerk, as if someone had fired a gunshot into each. All at once, the force binding him had been released. Without even realizing it, he had been tensing the muscles in his arms.

She was gone. He could sense it in the air. Feeling both startled at how easily she had given up and unnerved by the thought that he might have made her angry enough to try and get back at him, he lay there without moving.

9

The following day passed uneventfully, and the day of the engagement ceremony arrived.

This isn't over yet. There was no doubt in Tsuneo's mind about that. In fact, he felt so sure more was on the way that he began to think this certainty of his might be offering him a glimpse into his own heart. Could it be that, deep down inside, he was actually hoping he hadn't yet seen the end of it all?

He left the dorm at eleven in the morning.

If she's going to show up again, it will be today, the day of the ceremony. It was dumb of me to mention what time it's going to take place. I'll really have to watch out. I can't reply to the voice, no matter what it says – not there, in front of everyone. The thing that worried him was that each time she appeared she used a different method to get closer, so he hadn't the foggiest idea how to prepare himself.

He got to Yoshie's house a little after twelve-thirty. Director-General Saitō and his wife arrived about five minutes later.

* * *

Tsuneo's grandfather, who had passed away some fourteen years earlier, had sounded like a completely different person when he chanted sutras. That's how different the voice he used then was from his ordinary voice.

During summer vacation, when Tsuneo left Tokyo and went to stay at his grandfather's house in Matsusaka, Mie Prefecture, he used to hear the old man chanting at the altar every morning, and then again every night. That voice always seemed strange to him, no matter how many times he heard it. His grandfather ran a small shop that sold rice; he was a hefty, mild-mannered man who was constantly smiling and saying, 'Hmhn?' No matter what you said to him, he just smiled and nodded and said, 'Hmhn?' He offered no further comment on anything.

And yet when he recited the sutras, his voice sounded like a samurai's: thick and vibrant, with a strength that seemed to well up from somewhere deep inside. The old man's bent back straightened like a rod when he knelt down before the altar, and his voice grew so loud he sounded almost angry. At first, Tsuneo hadn't even realized the voice was his grandfather's. And even after he learned that it was, he still had a vague sense that his grandfather had some other person inside him, someone who only emerged when he chanted.

He remembered his grandfather at Yoshie's house on the day of the engagement ceremony, when, with no advance warning at all, Director-General Saitō suddenly sat up very straight and started speaking in a different voice.

They had all been chatting about this and that when he suggested that they begin, and as soon as he had made the suggestion, the smile he'd been wearing vanished without a trace, and his voice took on a new depth and resonance: 'Well then,' he boomed, 'without further ado . . .' Tsuneo started, thinking that the woman had done something, but he soon realized this wasn't the case. It was the Director-General's public occasions voice.

Yoshie and her parents were kneeling on one side, their feet tucked under them in the formal style; Mr and Mrs Saitō and Tsuneo knelt opposite them. The Director-General waited for everyone to start looking serious enough to match the change in his own voice and posture, then began once more: 'Without any further ado . . .' He was speaking so loudly he seemed to think he was in a hall or something, not an ordinary eight-mat room. It was a bit unusual, to be sure, but it had nothing to do with 'the woman with the voice'. This voice was one the Director-General carried within himself.

'I would like to commence this ceremony,' Director-General Saitō boomed, 'by means of which Tsuneo, eldest son of the Kasama family, will be formally engaged to Yoshie, eldest daughter of the Shibata family.'

At this, all at once, everyone lowered their heads.

Tsuneo glanced over at Yoshie as he raised his head and saw that she was raising hers too, slowly, with a very earnest look on her face. Her mother, who sat alongside her, and her father, who sat next to her mother in the place of honor, had both expunged all trace of emotion from their faces, and looked like entirely different people.

'Ordinarily, Tsuneo's father Kōichirō would have been expected to participate in this ceremony, but as various circumstances render this impossible, my wife Masako and I have taken it upon ourselves to accompany Tsuneo today, bringing these items betokening his engagement to your daughter, in the hope that we can deliver them unto you –' Saitō fell silent.

'Deliver them unto you' sounded strange. 'Which is to say,' he tried next, 'that it is in the hope that you might be gracious in accepting these items –' That sounded strange too, but he persevered: '– that we have all gathered here, as you know, today.' The words had become kind of jumbled up in his mouth. But Saitō didn't waver. No one else moved a muscle. 'That, I mean to say, is why we're here. Congratulations to everyone on this auspicious occasion!'

With that, Yoshie and her parents bowed their heads very low and cried out, all together and so loudly it gave Tsuneo a start, 'Thank you very much!'

They were all so earnest, and of course half the reason they were acting that way was to show respect for Tsuneo . . . Obviously it was inappropriate to find any of this at all amusing.

Just then, Mrs Saitō started to speak.

'This day –' Her tone was so solemn she sounded like a samurai's wife. Tsuneo, completely taken by surprise, had to clench his lips to keep from laughing. His nostrils flared. '– is a day for celebration. Congratulations.'

After lingering over these words, Mrs Saitō positioned her hands on the tatami mat and bowed. Tsuneo lowered his head at the same time. He had been instructed that the main thing was to be sure to lower and raise his head whenever Mr and Mrs Saitō raised and lowered theirs.

Mrs Saitō slowly got to her feet, then went over to the tray holding the symbolic engagement gifts, which included dried kelp, dried squid, and an elaborate decorative wrapper. She attempted to kneel before the tray, but lost her balance and ended up having to put her hands on the floor for a moment.

Everyone remained perfectly composed, however, as if they
hadn't even noticed what had happened. Mrs Saitō righted herself almost immediately, then picked up the tray and started to
stand up, holding the gifts straight out in front of her. She must
have got dizzy as she rose, though, because once again she lost
her balance, tottering as she took her first few steps.

Everyone gave an involuntary little cry when they saw this
and started to rise, but Mrs Saitō gave her buttocks a quick little
twist, as if she were dancing, and thus managed to keep the tray
level. Everyone faced forward again.

Tsuneo's nostrils flared as he clenched his lips again.

Mrs Saitō slowly made her way over to where Yoshie was
kneeling.

Yoshie rose part-way, backed up a little, and slid the cushion
on which she had been sitting to one side.

Mrs Saitō knelt down. So did Yoshie.

Mrs Saitō raised the tray holding the gifts up over her head for
a moment, then set it down on the tatami. Yoshie positioned both
hands in front of her on the tatami and made a very deep bow.

'What you see before you,' said Mrs Saitō, her voice as
solemn as before, 'are the engagement gifts Kasama Tsuneo has
brought for you. May you treasure them for years to come.'

'Thank you very much,' Yoshie replied, her tone equally the-
atrical. She sounded like a specialist in male roles from the
all-female Takarazuka acting troupe. 'I will treasure these gifts
for years to come.'

Mrs Saitō was saying something.

There's nothing funny here. Ceremonies are always like this.
Tsuneo was too old to be giggling at a ceremony. He actually
found it kind of sad. I have no right at all to laugh at this kind of

thing. Ceremony plays a bigger part in the life I'm living now than in most people's lives, and no doubt that will continue to be true. Even after this engagement ceremony is over, even after the wedding, I'm bound to go on acting the role I've been allotted, putting a lid on my emotions, just as we do on occasions like this.

All of a sudden Yoshie's parents called out in unison, 'Thank you very much!' They positioned their hands on the tatami and made a very deep bow. 'We greatly appreciate the trouble you have taken.'

For reasons of which he was hardly conscious, laughter welled up inside Tsuneo. Once more he tightened his lips; once more his nostrils flared.

Yoshie stared at him, evidently surprised. Her parents, kneeling beside her, were looking at him too, their mouths slightly agape.

'Hey, Kasama!' Mr Saitō called his name, loudly.

But he couldn't answer. His expression was distorted. He was laughing. He couldn't stop. He covered his face with the palms of his hands, pressing hard, and doubled over in an effort to contain it, but his whole frame shook and a gasp of laughter trickled out. It's the woman with the voice! The woman with the voice! She's responsible for this! he thought, trying to look serious, but as hard as he tried to stop it, the laughter just kept coming. He'd been overcome by a feeling of amusement several times since the ceremony had begun. He should have tried harder to restrain himself from the start. He'd just assumed the feeling was natural. But come to think of it, there was something weird about the way he was reacting. Really, there was nothing funny about any of this. The matchmaker at his engagement had started speaking in a loud voice without any warning, and his wife had lost her balance and ended up on all fours . . . that wasn't funny. Yoshie looked awfully serious didn't she? But then on the other hand . . . maybe it really *was* natural for him to be amused by these things? Maybe the really ridiculous thing is to keep a straight face when such ridiculous things are taking place?

'You insolent wretch!' Mr Saitō was shouting.

'Don't!' Mrs Saitō shook her head violently from side to side. 'Darling!'

'Mr Saitō . . .' Yoshie's father was half standing up, gesturing uncertainly.

The voices of Mr Saitō, his wife, and Yoshie's parents were all mixed up together. Mr Saitō kicked Tsuneo, who had collapsed onto the floor, in the stomach.

'This is a celebration!' screamed Mrs Saitō. 'A celebration! Darling!'

Very slowly, Tsuneo rose to his feet. The laughter had vanished, as though some tricky fox that had possessed him had finally let go.

'You should apologize, Mr Kasama! Apologize to the matchmaker!'

'That's right! Tell him you're sorry!'

Yoshie's parents were yelling. He didn't hear Yoshie say anything.

'Please accept my apologies!' Tsuneo shouted. He put his hands on the tatami and made a deep bow. I can't let the woman with the voice beat me, he thought.

'No sense of decency, this kid. He's a joker!'

Tsuneo had his gaze directed at the floor, but he could see

Mr Saitō's black socks out of the corner of his eye. His boss was stamping his foot.

'He said he's sorry,' said Mrs Saitō. 'Isn't that enough?'

'Who the hell does he think this ceremony is for!'

'Forgive me!' Tsuneo raised his voice to match that of his boss.

'Please forgive him, Mr Saitō!'

'Yes, please! Please!'

Yoshie's parents got on their knees beside Tsuneo and placed their hands before them on the tatami.

'There's no need for you two to apologize.' Mr Saitō's voice was still quivering. 'This has nothing to do with you.'

'Before long he'll be our son, and we'll be his parents. Part of the responsibility lies with us,' cried Yoshie's father. Yoshie's mother picked up where he left off: 'Yes, yes, it's our fault too!'

'What are you talking about?' muttered Mr Saitō, evidently annoyed. 'You two haven't done anything. Kasama's the problem!'

'I'm sorry!' Tsuneo screamed once more.

'Yoshie! Why are you just sitting there like that? You ought to apologize too!' said Yoshie's mother.

'Ha! Why should I?' This was the first time Yoshie had opened her mouth.

'What do you mean, why should you?' shouted her father, furious. 'This man is going to be your husband!'

'Yeah, but I can't apologize if I haven't done anything, can I?'

'Don't get nitpicky with me! Just say you're sorry!'

'Say you're sorry, Yoshie!' Yoshie's mother chimed in.

'Now, now, there's no need for that.' Mrs Saitō's tone was conciliatory. 'Really, there's no need for Yoshie to apologize. It's okay, dear.' The Saitōs had been living in the house next to Yoshie's for about four years, so they were good friends. 'And I must say,' she went on, turning to her husband, 'I think you're being very childish. What point is there in making Yoshie apologize?'

'When did I ever say that?' protested Mr Saitō, sounding a bit hurt. 'I never asked her to apologize!'

'Laughter is . . . it's a physiological phenomenon,' said Mrs Saitō to her husband, as though she were trying to make him see the light. 'There's no point getting so worked up about it.'

'It's true, really,' said Yoshie's father. 'This kind of thing happens. Sometimes people start laughing even though there's nothing funny at all, and then they simply can't stop.'

'I don't buy that,' said Mr Saitō. 'Laughter is never just a purely physiological phenomenon. He's a slacker. It's a mental thing.'

'I'm sorry!' Tsuneo screamed again.

'All right, that's enough!' said Mrs Saitō. 'These things happen.'

'These things *do not* happen!' Mr Saitō raised his voice again slightly. 'These things absolutely *do not* happen!'

'But it's fine if he laughs,' said Yoshie's father. 'I mean, depending on how you look at it, you could even say it's an auspicious sign if someone can't stop laughing at a celebration like this.'

'That's so true!' said Mrs Saitō. 'It's so much better than crying.'

'Really,' Yoshie's mother went on, 'much better than getting angry, too.'

Mrs Saitō picked up from there. 'You're absolutely right,' she said. 'It's really too awful for you to be shouting on a joyful occasion like this.'

'Oh no, no!' Yoshie's mother said, flustered. 'That's not what I meant at all!'

'You're right. You're quite right,' said Mr Saitō. His tone of voice made it clear that he had finally got hold of himself. 'It's okay, this has gone on long enough. You can lift your head, Kasama. I should have been a little more mature myself.'

'You certainly should have!' said Mrs Saitō, nodding vigorously.

'But come on, who laughs at a time like this?'

'I'm very sorry!' Tsuneo cried out an apology once more, his head still down. And then, all of a sudden, his eyes were filling with tears.

'Yoshie,' called her mother, 'we'd better bring out the trays.'

'I've got to apologize,' said Yoshie's father. 'We really don't have enough space in our house, so I'm afraid we're going to have to ask you to move into the sitting room for a few moments while we set up for lunch.'

'You too, Tsuneo,' said Yoshie's mother. 'You just go along into the next room with Mr Saitō.'

But Tsuneo didn't move.

'Come along in here, Mr Kasama,' said Mrs Saitō.

'I'm coming.'

He couldn't move. His eyes were filled with tears. He remained with his hands spread on the tatami, unable to lift his face, fighting down the sobs that kept welling up inside him. Damn her. Damn the woman with the voice. He knew it was her. He knew it, but he couldn't resist.

'It's okay, everything's okay now. No need to cry. Come on in here,' said Mrs Saitō, patting his shoulder.

Biting his lips, Tsuneo went into the next room.

'It's okay. That's enough,' said Mr Saitō. 'You're not a child.'
But he couldn't keep the sobs down.

He felt so sorry for all the people there. It made him so sad
to think that humans lived in this way, holding ceremonies like
this, as if it were entirely natural. The parents trying to convince
themselves that it's no big deal if the man their daughter is
about to marry bursts out laughing during the engagement
ceremony; the sulking Yoshie herself, who offered no response;
the outraged Mr Saitō and his wife, berating her husband for his
anger; and Tsuneo himself . . . the whole thing just made him
feel so forlorn and sad that before he realized what was happening he had burst into tears.

'Haven't we had enough of this already?' said Mr Saitō,
stunned.

'Mr Kasama!' said Mrs Saitō, kneeling right next to him and
slapping the tatami with her hand. 'You have no reason to cry!
You saw that you had done something inappropriate and you
apologized, right? That's all you needed to do. Stop crying.
Would you please stop crying?'

But just as he couldn't stop laughing before, he couldn't stop
crying now.

'Hit me, please,' cried Tsuneo through his sobs. 'Please, hit
me again.'

Maybe if he hits me I'll be able to stop, just as I did when I
was laughing.

'I can't hear you,' said Mrs Saitō. 'I can't understand you
when you're crying.'

'You understand all right,' said Mr Saitō. 'He's saying to hit
him.'

'How is it going to help, after all this, for him to hit you?

This is an engagement ceremony! Do you really think a match-maker can hit a future bridegroom like that? Or are you planning to hit him? Are you going to hit him?'

'Like hell I am! I've had enough of this.'

'See, he says it's enough. Don't make things any more difficult for us than you already have. What are you thinking? I mean, just as we're all saying it's better to laugh than to cry, you go and start crying. Stop it right now. Stop crying!'

But the sobs wouldn't stop.

Mr Saitō and his wife fell silent, evidently at a loss as to what to do.

Yoshie and her parents didn't say anything either. They just kept setting up the table in the next room, covering it with a plastic white tablecloth.

Tsuneo's voice – the cries that escaped as he tried to contain his sobbing – was the only sound that could be heard.

Then, quietly, Yoshie's mother spoke.

'Bring the beer in first, Yoshie. Just the beer.'

Yoshie, who had been standing there motionless, plodded off toward the kitchen. But her feet came to a stop when she was only part-way there.

'What's going on here?' she groaned, her voice so heavy it sounded as though she were pushing it up from the very bottom of her stomach.

'What?' Even from the next room, it was obvious that Yoshie's mother had just cast a startled glance in her daughter's direction.

'What the hell is going on here?' Yoshie shouted.

'Stop!' Her father immediately raised his voice, trying to keep her from saying anything more. 'You think it's going to help if you start talking that way too?'

'What the hell is up with this guy?' Yoshie glared down at Tsuneo from where she stood. 'I mean, what the hell! This whole thing is a fiasco! What's happening here! Isn't the matchmaker going to take responsibility for this?'

'How can you say such a stupid thing?' shouted her mother.

'Who's being stupid? Who's being stupid!' Yoshie cried at the top of her lungs. Then, running over to the alcove, she started grabbing the gifts and throwing them around the room. 'This is all crap! It's crap!'

'Yoshie!'

'Yoshie darling!'

Tsuneo knelt there trembling amidst all the shouting, trying to control his sobs.

Damn her. Damn that woman with the voice.

10

Director-General Saitō's driving was smooth and even, without a wasted movement. It struck Tsuneo that he himself would never have been able to remain so composed after all that had happened. On the other hand, Mr Saitō hadn't said a single word for the first twenty minutes after they left Yoshie's house. Just now they were merging onto the Shuto Expressway from the Yōga entrance. Mr Saitō had said he'd drive him to his dorm, in Edogawa ward. Tsuneo had declined the offer, only to be told, in a tone that sounded like a command, that it was no trouble, so get in. Mrs Saitō had remained at Yoshie's house.

If he'd been the matchmaker, he doubted it would even have occurred to him to drive the future groom to his dorm, not after he had caused such a ruckus. He would have told him to find his own damn way home. Tsuneo hadn't asked Mr Saitō to take on the role of matchmaker. It had been Mr Saitō's idea to go talk with Yoshie's parents, to tell them that there was a 'serious, likeable young man' in the office with 'a warm side' to him who might make a good match for Yoshie. Mrs Saitō must be having a miserable time right now. When Mr Saitō led Tsuneo out to the car, he had heard her muttering to herself at her husband's back, repeating the same phrases: 'I don't understand it at all, I really don't.' 'I mean, he's not usually like that . . .' Even now she was probably bowing to Yoshie and her parents, offering her apologies. He felt sorry for all the trouble he'd caused.

Mr Saitō only finally opened his mouth after they had passed Shibuya, some time after they emerged from the Aoyama Tunnel.

'Kasama.'

'Yes, sir?' By then, the tremor that had remained in Tsuneo's voice even after he stopped sobbing was gone.

'Put on your seatbelt.'

'Yes, sir.'

The Director-General fell silent for another twenty minutes or so. Maybe Tsuneo should have said something. 'What I did was terrible. Please accept my apologies. I know I've dragged your good name, and that of your wife, through the mud.' But he had the feeling it might sound glib. He figured it would be more appropriate to act as though he were so crushed he'd lost the ability to speak. If he were really feeling sorry for what he had done, and feeling it from the heart, he wouldn't have had the composure to try and decide what sort of attitude to take. He really did feel, though, that it hadn't been his fault. Damn that woman with the voice.

I've betrayed my boss's good will.

The question is, then, why is he driving me home like this? If he were just doing what came naturally to him, he probably wouldn't even want to see my face. I guess he's just keeping his emotions in check, trying to behave in a way he thinks appropriate for a boss and matchmaker. Except his anger is so strong that keeping it in check and driving the car at the same time is all he can manage: he's too busy to talk.

Traffic grew heavy as they approached Ryōgoku. Finally, as they sat there in the stopped car, Mr Saitō spoke again.

'You know . . .' His voice was calm.

'Yes, sir?'

'I used to be a security officer myself, so I sort of understand.'

'Yes, sir.' Tsuneo had a sense that it might not be wise to ask just what it was his boss sort of understood, so he simply nodded in agreement.

'Often, when you're working in immigration, it's hard to think of the people we go after as criminals.'

'Yes, sir.'

'Sometimes it gets to be too much.'

'Yes, sir.'

'It's my fault too for not noticing. But you know, if you're having problems, we could have postponed the engagement ceremony.'

'I really caused a lot of trouble, I know, and –'

'Look, it's okay. Just try and get some sleep tonight. Tomorrow we can go see a doctor together.'

'That's all right. I can go on my own.'

'Do you know a good doctor?'

'Yes. I went to see one once before . . .'

'Oh, I see . . .'

'That time he said there was nothing wrong.'

'Had something happened, then?'

'I felt like I couldn't control myself.' He couldn't bring himself to talk about the graveyard. 'And I felt sad about a whole lot of things.'

'I had that too. Some of these illegal immigrants are real sad cases. Sometimes even when you're trying not to feel anything, you just can't stand it anymore.'

'Yes, sir.'

'Yeah,' said Mr Saitō, sounding like a man calling up memories of the past as he slowly drove the car forward a little. 'That happened to me too.'

'Yes . . . sir.'

'You're worn out, that's all. Take two or three days off, starting tomorrow. I'll let the Chief Security Officer know.'

'No, that's all right. I can . . .'

'It's conscientious guys like you who end up getting sick. Forget about work. And for the time being we'll put a hold on talk about marriage. Unless that girl throws a fit, it'll be best to keep going as planned. I don't know, though . . .'

'It's perfectly natural for her to be angry.'

'She won't be much of a comfort if she's going to be that way.'

'No, sir.'

'It's true, though, isn't it? Once you start thinking things are sad, there's no end to it. Everything people do makes you sad.'

Once more silence descended upon the car. They got off the expressway at the Ichinoe interchange, took Kanshichi to Kuramaebashi Road, and turned right.

'You want me to send someone?' Mr Saitō asked as they drew near the dorm.

'No, I can manage alone. I just need to calm down.'

'Are you sure you're going to be okay?'

'I'll be fine. I've calmed down now.'

'What about getting in touch with your father?'

'He'd be too busy to do anything even if I did, so . . .'

Mr Saitō knew very well that his father had remarried, and his relationship with his son was such that he hadn't even come to the engagement ceremony.

'Oh.'

'I'm feeling so nervous today, something must have gone wrong with my wiring. I'm afraid I caused your wife a lot of trouble too.'

Mr Saitō questioned Tsuneo once more as he got out of the car at the dorm.

'So you're sure you can go see the doctor by yourself?'

'I'm sure. Thank you very much for everything.'

As the Director-General's Accord moved off into the distance, Tsuneo realized that at some point along the way he'd started acting, totally seriously, the role of a patient.

Only this wasn't a disease. He'd made the mistake of telling the woman with the voice the date and time at which the engagement ceremony was to take place. He had wondered what sort of attack she might launch, but never in his wildest dreams would laughter have occurred to him. And after that, everybody's favorite: sorrow. She had put a lot of effort into this.

'Come on out!' No sooner was Tsuneo inside than he shut the door and shouted. In his heart, that is. It was the weekend. The guy from the Ministry of Agriculture, Forestry, and Fisheries might be home. He didn't want to be disturbed. 'Come on out! Listen, wherever you are! Do you have any idea what you did today!'

He listened. He listened with his heart. There was no response.

'You can't do this. Don't try to play the innocent with me, not after all you did!'

'—'

He had a feeling she'd said something. He'd been yelling, so he couldn't be sure. He had the sense that the air around him had grown just a tiny bit denser.

'You hardly know anything about me. And yet, as little as you know, you make up your mind that you don't want me to be happy. You ruined my engagement!'

He could tell she was listening. It wasn't as if she was in the room. She was far, far away, but concentrating on his voice. That's how it felt.

'You must be delighted now that everything worked out just as you hoped.'

'*Did I . . .*'

Finally he heard her voice.

'Don't talk to me in that sorry tone! Speak in a way that fits what you did.'

'*Did I . . .*' said the voice again, this time with a faintly confrontational edge. This is more like it. It's a lot better than letting her keep calm. '*Did I destroy your happiness?*'

'I have pretty much no hope of getting married now.'

'*Does that mean I destroyed your happiness?*'

'I can't believe you're even saying that! Of course it does!'

'*All I did was think.*'

'Think what? Let it all be destroyed?'

'*No.*'

'You didn't give us your blessing, that's for sure. All you did was think? Just a little thinking, that's all? Okay, maybe that's true. But you know, whether you realize it or not, you've got power. You have the power to ruin people's lives. The simple fact that we're talking together like this proves that. Not just anyone can do this, you know. And the power that makes this possible is yours, not mine. Maybe this is nothing but a little twinge of jealousy as far as you're concerned. Maybe you're half-enjoying it. But everything's gone topsy-turvy on my end. So tell me, what is it you were thinking?'

'*I was just hoping you would be honest about your feelings.*'

'At one o'clock today?'

There was no response.

'At one o'clock today, of all times?'

'*Yes.*'

'That's not just thinking. Clearly you had bad intentions.'

'*A little . . .*'

'Not a little. I was in the middle of a formal engagement ceremony! You want me to be honest about my feelings at a time like that?'

'*What happened?*'

'You really don't know?'

'*I don't know.*'

'I told you the engagement is off.'

'*How did that happen?*'

'How do you think?'

'*You felt hatred.*'

'For whom?'

'*The woman.*'

'Why would I hate the woman I'm getting engaged to?'

'*There was something you didn't like about her.*'

'Why wouldn't I like her? You don't get engaged to someone you don't like.'

'*What was it, then? What happened?*'

'I laughed. The process of going through all the stages of the ceremony started to seem funny to me, and I burst out laughing. It was absolutely disgraceful. Sure, ceremonies can be kind of humorous from a certain point of view. Sometimes you can't help laughing to yourself at what's happening, it's true. But no one in his right mind lets it show. You're not being dishonest when you keep something like that to yourself. And then, all on account of you, I had those pathetic true feelings dragged out into the open. I was laughing my head off!'

'*I had no idea.*'

'You had no idea? How can you say that?'

'*I . . .*'

'What did you think would happen?'

'*Listen to me.*'

'I mean, sometimes the opening remarks start to feel long or you notice that your feet have fallen asleep . . . it happens to everyone on these occasions. But you have to keep that stuff to yourself.'

'*The chances that you care for her seem . . .*'

'Of course I cared about her!'

'*I was wondering, though . . . how you feel about her . . .*'

'And what business is that of yours?'

'*Why were you the one to hear my voice, not someone else . . .*'

'I haven't the slightest idea.'

'*I think it's because you're unhappy.*'

'It doesn't matter what you think.'

'*You didn't hate her. You didn't dislike her. You weren't happy with her. You didn't really feel anything at all for her.*'

'The way you're talking, you'd think you've just won at some game. Look, it was an arranged marriage! We met for the first time less than two months ago. It would be strange if I *was* sitting around thinking about her all the time.'

'*Why would you get married like that?*'

'Things are bound to work out better if they start that way. Marriages last longer if the bride and groom have a fairly clear idea of what they're getting into than if they get married when they're both crazy about each other, and reality only begins to set in afterwards, little by little. Look, it doesn't matter. You have no right to stick your nose into this in the first place, no matter what kind of marriage is scheduled. And I certainly don't see what right you have to ruin it all.'

'*Why are you the only one who is able to hear my voice?*'

'How would I know?'

'*I'm a very lonely person.*'

'There are lonely people all over the place.'

'*There's something you're trying to get over, I'm sure of it.*'

'You give me too much credit. I don't have anything to deal with – no wealth, no debts. I'm an utterly unremarkable man. I just want to have a peaceful household in some little corner of the world, that's all.'

'*Who's Eric?*'

'I've never heard of him.'

'*You said his name.*'

'I forget.'

'*No.*'

'Go away! Don't ever talk to me again. You understand me? I'm not going to answer anymore. No matter what you say or how you come at me, I'll resist you. Don't screw up my life any more than you already have! And if you don't lay off, I'm going to find out who you are. I'll track you down, and I'll do as much to you as you've done to me. Leave me alone. Go away, okay? Leave!'

He was shouting. He'd become so agitated that it wasn't enough to shout inside his heart. He thought there might be a knock on the door, but it was quiet.

The woman's voice vanished. Perhaps there had been the usual shift in the air, he didn't know. He was so wound up he was completely unable to sense such atmospheric subtleties. He slipped out of his jacket and undid his tie.

Be honest? Honest with my own feelings? *'You didn't feel anything at all for her.'* What the hell? I mean, sure, maybe that's true, but we were right in the middle of a ceremony, and that's how ceremonies are. Come to think of it, I didn't really feel any big rush of emotion – I wasn't wondering how Yoshie felt, I wasn't thinking that we were taking a big step toward marriage. But aren't most men like that?

He took off the pants of his best suit and hung them on their hanger, then flopped down on the bed in his underwear.

Yoshie. I wonder what she's doing now. And how she's feeling. He tried to put himself in her place, but nothing came to mind. Nothing happened in his heart, either. No rush of emotion. At the end of the day, he thought, staring at the ceiling, it's true, my feelings for her didn't run any deeper than that. But I was going to go ahead and marry her anyway. I guess I was being sort of ridiculous, shouting like that at the woman with the voice, making it sound as if my one shot at happiness had been ruined. Maybe I made a bit of a fool of myself.

It's true I wasn't expecting much from my marriage with Yoshie, even at the start, but that had nothing to do with her; I just don't think marriage amounts to much. Actually, it's not just marriage – I tend to view life the same way. An existence that looks pretty comfortable to others often isn't all that much in the eyes of the one actually living it. That's reality, I thought. And having recognized that, I decided to do with my life the same thing everyone else does with theirs. So I won't really be too hurt if this marriage falls through. I feel bad for Yoshie and her parents, but it's not like she's in love with me or anything, right? So she probably won't be too deeply wounded. Either way, it's my own fault, so I'll just have to apologize. I wonder if she might forgive me if I ask her to keep the ring?

Maybe things have turned out for the best. Maybe it's better to feel a little more emotionally involved in a marriage. I was probably taking too dark a view of things. I figured my life would be more or less the same no matter who I married, but on the other hand it's not terribly realistic to assume all women are the same. There are all sorts of women out there, right, so there are bound to be all sorts of marriages, and if that's the case, well then, who's to say I might not actually have a shot at a life with someone so happy it's like a dream come true – even if the chances of that happening are only one in ten thousand? Maybe I should be a little more willing to wait for that sort of miracle to happen? The kind of marriage where I'm thinking *this is the one*, and the feeling doesn't change after we're married, not even after a year, or five years, or ten years, and she feels the same way about me, and . . . What the hell are you talking about, man? If a marriage like that ever existed, it'd only exist because both of the parties involved were out of their minds! They'd just be running from reality. A couple so insufferably sentimental you couldn't stand to be around them – that's what they'd be, no doubt about it. Enough of the stupid dreams. If I sat around waiting for that miracle to happen, I'd end up letting even the ordinary sort of happiness most people enjoy slip away from me. Linking my lot with Yoshie's was a perfectly realistic course of action. The damned woman! Damn that woman with the voice! How am I supposed to go on living, now that you've destroyed all that?

'*Why does it have to be that way?*'

Tsuneo gave a start. She's still here. He wouldn't reply. He held his breath.

'*Why are you so set against dreaming?*'

He didn't move.

'*Why are you so convinced that reality is a bore?*'

He made up his mind not to think at all.

'*Hello? I know you can hear me.*'

He tried to think of something else. Oh yeah. That guy who joined the bureau the same year I did, Kawai, is supposed to be returning from his stint at the Japanese embassy in Djakarta tomorrow. Two years earlier, it had been suggested that Tsuneo might go and work at the embassy in Bangkok. He had declined the offer on the pretext that Hamano, who'd joined the bureau the year after him, was dying to go. The truth was he didn't want to live abroad.

'*Why?*' the woman was saying. '*Why have you so completely given up? What is it that makes you think reality is so dull?*'

I haven't given up. It's just that reality really *is* dull. What can I do? There's no helping it, because this is the only reality I've encountered.

'*I decided that even if it is . . .*'

What should I do about my promise to Mr Saitō? I told him
I'll go see a doctor tomorrow. Will it be enough just to tell him I
went? To tell him the doctor says there's nothing wrong?

'Even if it is like that, I . . .'

And what should I do about Yoshie's family? Can I get by
without apologizing? I guess I should probably go. Should I go
tomorrow? Is it even okay for me to go by myself? Should I talk
to Mr Saitō first?

'I decided I would dream.'

It depends on whether or not I want to go through with this
marriage. If I'm willing to let it fall to pieces, I should go with
Mr Saitō. Hold on a second, is that right? I'm not sure it is. On
the other hand, if I go alone I might end up giving the impression that I'm sorrier about what happened than I really am.
There's a chance Yoshie might start to cry. They'll end up saying
what's done is done. She and I will get married. Is that really
what I want?

'No, it's not.'

'Look, you don't know what you're talking about!'

'I made a wish. I wished and a miracle happened.'

'A miracle?'

'Yes.'

'Like what?'

'I'm talking to you.'

'You think this is a miracle?'

*'If it's not a miracle, what is it? I wished for this from the bottom
of my heart. Wished that someone out there would be open to these
feelings of mine. Day after day after day, I kept gazing up into the
sky, calling out, "Hello? Hello?"'*

'Didn't work.'

'*What?*'

'Your miracle-inducing machine was on the blink. Your voice reached the wrong person entirely. The guy who heard it doesn't have the time to listen, and as far as he's concerned, your miraculous intervention is nothing but a nuisance.'

'*Do you mean that?*'

'You say you were gazing up into the sky day after day, calling out "Hello" in that pitiful voice of yours? Give me a break! The message that made it through to me wasn't like that at all. It was an assault on the lower half of my body of a variety I hesitate even to mention. Your transmitting tube must have been broken. The nature of the message changed.'

'*No.*'

'It wasn't like you called me the next time, either. That was a violent attack, so rough I had no chance of resisting.'

'*It was all me – I did all that. Because no matter how I poured my heart into those calls, they never reached anyone.*'

'Ordinarily people would find that perfectly natural.'

'*I hurled my whole being into the sky. Everything in me.*'

'Really? Look, saying that stuff just doesn't cut it. It was a sudden, massive wind. Like a tropical storm, maybe, or a boiler exploding.'

'*I knew it had reached someone.*'

'That's all you have to say for yourself? I had to go into the toilet at that temple, I was in a panic, and that's all you can say?'

'*What happened?*'

'You know what happened, you're just forcing me to say it.'

'*I wouldn't do that.*'

'You have the nerve to say that? Think about the feeling you hit me with.'

'*Why was that the only feeling that made it?*'

'That's always been the one that gets through to men the easiest.'

'*I wanted to show you that there's more to me as a woman than that.*'

'That explains what happened that night?'

'*What was it like?*'

'You're the one who made it happen.'

'*I just directed my feelings toward you, giving it all I had. That's all.*'

'You made me burst into tears.'

'*Why?*'

'As if I'd know. You made me cry. I felt sad for no reason.'

'*It made me happy.*'

'Making me cry?'

'*I didn't know I'd made you cry. I just felt that someone had been open to the feelings I was sending.*'

'I wasn't open to them. I was swept away by them.'

'*I was engrossed in my questioning. What are you like? Tell me who you are?*'

'All I heard was "Who are you?" Off in the distance. I didn't have time to reply. You were already gone.'

'*I got tired.*'

'I got tired too.'

'*But a channel was opened. We can talk. I'm glad I didn't give up. I kept thinking how wonderful it would be if I could talk to someone like this.*'

'What sort of illness is it?'

'*Illness?*'

'You must have been sick for a long time.'

'*No.*'

'Then you're walled in on all sides by concrete.'

'*Hmmph. In a solitary cell serving a life sentence?*'

'I'm not saying that much. I don't know how long you're in for.'

'*I could leave right now.*'

'Then I have no idea who you are.'

'*A mystery woman.*'

'It won't help you to put on airs. I'm not the slightest bit interested.'

'*It's true. I'm tired. Because you're half turned away. Because . . . you don't . . . turn . . . to face . . . me.*'

Tsuneo started choosing his next words, but already she was gone. Of course he wasn't facing her! She sticks her nose in where she's not wanted, appearing to a man who's telling her to leave, and then when he starts talking to her because he has no choice she doesn't thank him, no, she complains that 'you don't turn to face me' and vanishes all of a sudden. He hated that type of woman more than anything.

'Don't come again,' he said quietly, doubting that she would hear.

There was no answer.

He noticed that the room was growing dark. Dusk had fallen. God, I sure talked with her a long time. What an idiot I am.

11

Tsuneo arrived at the office at eight-forty the following morning.

It wouldn't be right to take the day off without even asking, relying on the Director-General to take care of things. Besides, he didn't need a day off. On the other hand, he'd made things pretty difficult for Mr Saitō, so he couldn't very well act as though nothing whatsoever were wrong. It's probably best to tell him I was exhausted and my nerves were shot. I'll have to see the doctor this afternoon, I suppose – that much is unavoidable. But he didn't want to do any more than that, not if it would get in the way of work.

When he entered the room, Sakuma and the rest of them were gathered around Miyazaki, chuckling.

'What's so funny?' he said, smiling at them as he closed the door.

'Oh-ho!' bellowed Miyazaki. 'It's written all over your face!'

'What are you talking about?'

'You had the engagement ceremony, no?'

Miyazaki had some nerve, teasing his superior. Even if they had entered the bureau in the same year.

Tsuneo replied, 'None of your business', but by then Sakuma and the others were making such a ruckus that his voice was drowned out: 'Hey, yeah!' 'That's right, I'd forgotten!' 'Congratulations!'

'You guys sure are lively today,' said Tsuneo, fending off their voices. 'What's going on?'

'It's Maeda,' Sakuma told him.

Apparently a very cute Filipino girl had come in to thank Inspector Maeda. She had been brought in on a raid, but it turned out she'd been the victim of a fraud, and as a student she had been able to extend her period of residence.

'What, did she kiss him or something?'

'People aren't *that* enamoured of immigration officers!' cried Sakuma gleefully, evidently imitating Maeda, who tended to be extraordinarily uptight. Maeda himself added, 'Quite right.' Chief Security Officer Honda walked in at that point, having arrived at the office slightly late. He seemed puzzled to see Tsuneo there.

They worked until a little past ten o'clock on the arrangements for an upcoming raid on a 'bathhouse' in Taito ward. As soon as the meeting was over, Tsuneo went to look in at the General Affairs Division, only to learn that Director-General Saitō had gone to the Ministry of Justice.

Tsuneo was scheduled to scout out a site that afternoon, so he had been hoping to see Mr Saitō in the morning to say thank you and offer his apologies once more for the previous day, but that wouldn't work if his boss was out of the office.

He was just about to head back to his own area when Mr Honda opened the door of the Chief of Security's Office and called his name. 'Hey, Kasama!'

Come to think of it, when Mr Saitō told me to take time off yesterday, he had said he'd explain things to Mr Honda. I ought to have gone up to Mr Honda earlier and told him everything was fine, so I came to work after all.

The Chief of Security was out, and Mr Honda was sitting in a chair in the waiting room. 'Weren't you going to stay home today?' he asked.

'You heard from the Director-General?' replied Tsuneo, taking a seat on the chair Mr Honda had indicated.

'Yeah,' said Mr Honda, averting his gaze. 'I got a call from him last night.'

'It's nothing at all, really. I'm fine.'

'No doubt, but you should go see a doctor all the same.'

'Yes, sir.'

'It's the disease of modernity. Could happen to anyone.'

'Yes, sir.'

'I had a letter of introduction prepared. It's for a place in Aoyama Rokuchōme.' Mr Honda held out a thin envelope. It was addressed to the doctor at the clinic and signed by the Chief of Security, Mr Kamihara. 'Will you be all right going on your own?'

'I'll be fine.'

'You'd get there during lunch if you left now. What if I call and tell them you'll be there at one?'

'I'm supposed to scout out a site this afternoon.'

'Don't worry about it. Take some time off.'

'I don't know what the Director-General told you, but this really isn't a big deal. I don't even think it's necessary for me to go to this clinic. I just figured there was no other way for me to set people's minds at ease, that's all . . . it's not anything that will interfere with my work. I'll go see the doctor, but I want to participate in the raid tonight.'

'Either way, the doctor comes first.' Mr Honda stood up, as if to put an end to the conversation. His manner wasn't exceptionally cold, but Tsuneo felt a little hurt all the same. Mr Honda was a man who loved talent. He behaved coldly toward those who didn't have it. He was never blatant about it, but he had a tendency to ignore the duller members of his staff. Tsuneo himself had never been treated this way by Mr Honda, but from time to time he had sensed that it was happening to one or another of his co-workers.

'From now on, follow the doctor's orders.'

'Yes, sir.'

The door had already closed. Tsuneo could hear Mr Honda's footsteps moving down the hall. It seemed to him that, for the first time in his life, he had been treated as someone who is useless. Hey, hey, aren't you being a little over-sensitive? Maybe this is just the power of suggestion? I'm not going a little weird in the head, am I? Tsuneo got to his feet, staring at the closed door, and gave a forced, sour grin.

* * *

The clinic was on the sixth floor of a building near Aoyama Gakuin University. Tsuneo spent almost an hour and a half there, talking with a doctor who appeared to be in his late fifties. A young woman dressed in white who didn't look at all like a nurse sat off to the side, transcribing their conversation. He was asked to give a brief account of his life, beginning in childhood, and to discuss his relationship with his family – he had done all this previously when he went to see the other psychiatrist on his own initiative. As he explained that he had no siblings, his

mother had died, and his father had remarried, he came per-
ilously close to saying that none of this had anything to do with
anything, and telling the doctor about the woman with the
voice.

He'd probably think I'm completely nuts if I told him that,
though. There's no way anyone would ever believe such a story.

He answered the doctor's questions as they came, telling
him how delighted he was that his father had remarried; then,
during a pause in the conversation, he offered his own analysis
of the situation.

'To tell you the truth, I think I've been exhausted, that's all,'
he said. 'I just had a little trouble controlling my feelings.'

'Hmm.'

Tsuneo had made this same observation the moment he
sat down, and repeated it twice more during the course of
their talk. Each time the doctor had offered a vague response
that made it seem as though his thoughts were occupied by
other matters. Every once in a while he would abruptly flip two
or three pages in the binder he had in his hand, making a fair
amount of noise. Tsuneo found himself wondering about *his*
sanity. If you ask me, this guy seems a lot crazier than I am.

Just then, the doctor spoke again. 'Tell me now,' he purred,
suddenly adopting a very intimate tone, 'is it true you told
Yoshiko –'

'It's Yoshie.' The woman in white corrected him at once.
'Shibata Yoshie.'

'Is it true you told Yoshie about what happened?'

'What happening are you referring to?'

'About how you hear voices. A voice that says "Good
evening" and stuff.'

How does he know that? Who got that information from Yoshie? I suppose it must have been either Mr Saitō or his wife. Yoshie must have thought things over and decided there was something strange about me from the start. That's probably what she told them.

'That was just a joke.'

'Kind of an odd joke, isn't it?'

'I was drunk.'

The doctor flipped a few more pages in the binder, and then, once again, came out with something unexpected.

'The man next door, in your dorm . . .'

'Yes?'

'He says sometimes you start yelling and crying and so on.'

'Hold on, who –'

'The man living in the apartment next to yours, in the dorm.'

'I'm not asking that, I'm asking who went and questioned him.'

'That I don't know. I imagine your boss was concerned, so he went and asked around a bit.'

'But this whole thing only started yesterday!'

'They're great at what they do, these immigration people.'

Mr Saitō could have called the Ministry of Agriculture, Forestry, and Fisheries. Knowing that jerk next door, he would have been thrilled, told him everything: 'He was dripping with sweat . . .' '. . . very pale . . .' '. . . shouting . . .'

'Don't take it badly. He only did it out of concern for you.'

'I was practicing reading out loud.'

'Giving a talk somewhere, are you?'

'No. It's a hobby. I got carried away and raised my voice and that disturbed my neighbor. That's all it was.'

'I hear something happened on a raid?'

'Oh, that. That was just a screw-up on my part. The guy tripped me. It had nothing to do with what happened yesterday.'

As he was talking, Tsuneo realized that he had given Emoto from the Yokohama Branch Office a fairly detailed account of his experience in the graveyard. But they wouldn't have called the Yokohama office, would they? Besides, even if they did, Emoto wasn't the sort of guy who would repeat a story like that to someone's boss.

'For the time being, let's just say you need a week off to recuperate. Come and see me again the day after tomorrow. And take the medicine I've prescribed.'

'I don't need to take a whole week off.'

'What's wrong with giving yourself a vacation? There's no need for you to go all out for the great Japanese nation like this, you know. When you feel like taking a break you should take one, even if you have to bend the rules a bit to get it. Nothing will work out right unless you're the one deciding how you spend your days. You can't keep relying on work your whole life, you know. People who have nothing but work are weak. If they fail at their job, they have a hard time picking themselves up again.'

'My failure during that raid doesn't bother me.'

'I didn't get the impression that it did. Look, you yourself admitted that you've been feeling worn out. No one's going to hold it against you if you take a week off. Try to get some good sleep. And most important of all: absolutely do not start feeling desperate and try to *work* at taking it easy.'

Tsuneo was waiting for the medicine in the lobby when Mr Honda called.

'I spoke with the doctor. Follow his instructions, take some time off. You don't need to worry about anything. Come back to work when you're better. And make sure you take your medicine.'

His tone was sincere but a little overbearing. Mr Honda was a very rational sort of man, but sometimes in dealing with members of his staff he tried to play the role of the sentimentalist. Generally speaking, however, he only staged these little dramas with people he knew were susceptible; Tsuneo felt rather insulted to find himself being targeted. All right, enough! It's happening again, I'm getting paranoid in that weird way again. It's true, I guess I've been letting myself get carried away with work. I thought I was keeping my emotions under control – that's how I was supposed to be living my life – and here I am being thrown into a spin every time my boss changes his tone of voice! My self-image doesn't seem all that stable, does it? Since when did I get to be like this? Just another run-of-the-mill civil servant?

He walked to Shibuya.

That screw-up in the graveyard and the yelling in the dorm and the ugly spectacle he'd created during the engagement ceremony could all be attributed to 'the woman with the voice' – none of it had anything to do with his own mental state. And yet even as Tsuneo was blaming the voice, he found himself peering into the depths of his own heart. Perhaps, he thought, in some way no one else suspected, there was something wrong with him after all.

I was on the verge of getting married, feeling that it hardly mattered who the bride was. Maybe I was trying a bit too hard to keep myself from dreaming. I was running away from my own happiness. Isn't it about time, though, that I cut myself some slack? Can't I accept reality, admit that I'm just an ordinary civil servant, cultivate a few ordinary dreams, and try to find a wife who can live those dreams with me, at least to a certain extent? Shouldn't I be allowed to wish for that much happiness? Hasn't it been long enough now that even Eric should be willing to look the other way?

The gritty realities of his approaching marriage to Yoshie had been all too apparent, shining through all the pretty trappings . . . yes, he found himself thinking once again, it would be better if all that fell through. It's okay for me to dream a little more. Because some dreams do come true, at least in part. Not just in part, either – there's that woman with the voice, after all. To think something like that can really happen! The woman with the voice. On the other hand, though, can I really be sure she's not a hallucination, a creation of my own interior self?

'Can it be that I'm still not sure, even now?'

He made his way slowly down Miyaeki Hill.

Didn't I already confirm that she's real?

Turn to face this way –
Mine as well, this loneliness
The end of autumn.

If that voice actually did exist, then it meant he was in the middle of something monumental. And if it didn't, well, in that case he was still experiencing something monumental, it was just monumental in a personal sense. For him to be experiencing auditory hallucinations of such clarity, talking with the voice for so long . . . this was the sort of thing that happened to people when they were completely falling apart. Only he wasn't falling apart.

He walked into a small park that ran up against the back of a movie theater and a business hotel on one side and the elevated tracks of the Yamanote line on the other.

People were sitting on a few of the benches playing shōgi. Several men stood around them, looking on. Tsuneo took a seat on a bench a little distance away.

In front of him was a small flowerbed. Tired-looking red and yellow flowers were blooming there. It was heartbreaking to see them like that, as though they were being forced to blossom despite everything, in the sunless area behind the two buildings. Tsuneo averted his eyes.

The park was oddly quiet.

The area around it was brimming with the hubbub of the crowds and the furious flow of traffic, but there in that small park that smelled like a toilet, tiny sounds that could never survive outside this space – the scraping of a man's sandals on the ground when he shifted his position, for instance – could be heard.

He leaned back against the bench, stretched out, and gazed up at the sky. It was very blue, and there wasn't a cloud in sight. Though here in the park one had the impression it was cloudy.

'Hello?' Tsuneo aimed this at the sky. He didn't actually speak. He focused his feelings, spoke the words in the area around his chest.

It seemed to him this was the only thing he could do. He would spend his week-long vacation tracking down the woman.

'Hello? Hello?'

'*Yes?*' He heard the woman's voice.

'That was quick.' Tsuneo smiled.

'*I was waiting.*'

'You expected me to call?'

'*No, I didn't.*'

'Then why were you waiting?'

'*I was waiting for night. I figured you would be at work all day, so I thought I'd wait until night and then call you.*'

'I want you to promise me something.'

'*To promise . . .*'

'I'll tell you about Eric.'

'*About Eric?*'

'It's something I've never told anyone.'

'*Are you sure?*'

'In return, I want you to meet me.'

'—'

'You understand, right? The fact that we're talking like this isn't normal. I want to be sure you really exist. There's no way I'll be able to stand talking with you in this way unless I feel that certainty. I'll have no other choice but to assume there's something wrong with me. I need your help.'

'*Yes, but . . .*'

'I was the only one who heard your voice. Maybe that wasn't just chance.'

'*Yes.*'

'I think I'll be able to tell you about Eric.'

'*Yes, but . . .*'

'Tonight. Call me tonight. I'll tell you. Then – it can be tomorrow. It can be the day after that. I want to see you.'

There was no response.

'Hello? Hello?'

She was gone.

'Hey, kid.' All of a sudden someone called out to him from behind, a little off to one side. Tsuneo was so startled his whole body shook. It hadn't even occurred to him that anyone could be standing there. The truth was, until a moment ago no one was. 'Are you on drugs?' It was a rich, resonant voice.

'No, I am not on drugs.'

Glancing back, Tsuneo saw a man in his sixties or thereabouts sitting at the edge of a flowerbed directly behind his bench; the man had on a suit. Tsuneo had been expecting to see a homeless man, and was surprised to see him so sharply dressed.

'You were talking to yourself.' The man gave a little smile. 'You sounded really happy.'

'I didn't notice.' Tsuneo got to his feet, giving a sour smile.

'You're in pretty bad shape for someone your age, huh?'

'You should keep off the drugs too, old man.' It was all Tsuneo could do just to say this much. He started heading toward the railings.

'Old folks can do what they please. We've got nothing to fear.'

Tsuneo heard the man laughing triumphantly behind him.

12

Tsuneo was rather shocked to learn that he had been speaking out loud. He had told the woman to call him that night, but now he felt like getting in touch with her immediately, telling her about Eric, and then going right away to meet her and confirm that she wasn't simply a hallucination. He tried calling to her on the train – 'Hello?' – but received no response.

He called to her again once he was back in his room, mouthing the word 'Hello?' again and again in his heart. Still there was no answer.

He went to a convenience store to buy a boxed dinner. The whole way there and back, he kept listening for her.

Back at home again, he was given such a jolt by the loud ringing of the phone that he jumped.

'How are you doing?' asked Mr Saitō.

'I went to General Affairs this morning, but you were at the Ministry.'

'How about coming to our house tomorrow after six?'

'Yes, sir.'

'We have to make good use of this coming Sunday. I'll be in Fukuoka next week on work.'

'I'll come.'

'Yoshie is . . . well, you saw how she was acting. She's rushing to get everything settled. My wife says she'll talk to them all, if that's what you want.'

'But I'm the one who created all this trouble in the first place.'

'That's true, of course, but then on the other hand it's not as if you did anything terrible enough to make them break off the engagement, just like that. Yoshie hasn't been having much luck finding a marriage partner either, you realize. She's angry right now, but my wife says everything can be smoothed over, depending on how she handles the discussion.'

'It seems to me it might be best to let her keep the engagement ring to show her how sorry I am and then just to forget that any of this ever happened –'

'You sure give up easily, huh?'

'I've lost all my confidence.'

'Whatever. Come for dinner tomorrow. We'll talk then.'

'Thanks so much for everything.'

'Actually, about the ring . . . apparently Yoshie took it to Sangenjaya this morning, explained the situation, and had them buy it back for the same price you paid for it. You have to be quick with things like that, you know, otherwise they won't give you as much as you laid out. Yoshie's got a really good head for these things. To tell you the truth, that's what made me think she'd be a good match.'

'Yes, sir.'

'My wife is holding onto the three hundred thousand for you. Yoshie said she paid two hundred thousand of it herself?'

'Yes, sir.'

'She wants to return the three hundred thousand you contributed. She doesn't want any sort of compensation.

Apparently she was crying. She says she wants to forget any of this ever happened.'

'I understand.'

'She's not a bad kid. My wife thinks she'll be open to further discussion once she's calmed down.'

'I'll come and see you tomorrow.'

All at once Tsuneo felt terribly exhausted; he tumbled into bed. Only a day had passed and already she had changed the ring back into cash. Wasn't that just a little too fast? Had his behavior during the engagement ceremony been so grotesquely out of the ordinary that Yoshie could no longer even think of marrying him?

'The thing is, she's an extremely common sort of person.'

He had spoken these words aloud. This isn't good. I have to be careful or I'm just going to keep getting weirder and weirder.

It was a little past eleven that night when the woman finally called.

'*Hello?*'

'Finally. I was waiting, you know. I was waiting.'

Tsuneo sat up in bed.

'*Really?*'

'Yes, really. I called any number of times. Couldn't you hear me?'

'*I heard you, but –*'

'Then why didn't you answer?'

'*I was undecided.*'

'About what?'

'*I couldn't decide whether or not to meet you.*'

'You will, right?'

'—'

'You'll let me tell you about Eric, won't you?'

'*Meet me tomorrow at three-thirty, under the clock at Mullion, in Yūrakuchō*

'Thank you. I have no desire to try and sweet-talk you right now. I can't really say I care enough about you for that. I mean, after all, it hasn't been long since we first started getting acquainted. What I'm trying to say is that at the moment, this urge I have to confirm that you really do exist is uppermost in my mind, but . . . I have the feeling that if I tell you about Eric, you know, and if we keep interacting like that, in that way, eventually I'll find I have no choice but to consider you a very special person in my life.'

'*Start.*'

'Huh?'

'*Tell me about Eric.*'

'All right then, I will. I want to go to the bathroom first, though.'

'*Go right ahead.*'

'I could talk in the toilet too, of course, but I don't want to do that.'

'*I'll be waiting.*'

'Okay. I'll just tell you . . . you see, I failed my college entrance exams.'

'*When was that?*'

'About ten years ago.'

'*I see.*'

'Failed the next year too. Maybe I was aiming too high.'

'*Weren't you going to go to the bathroom?*'

'I don't want you to leave.'

'*Don't worry, I won't.*'
'Tomorrow at three-thirty, huh?'
The woman's voice gave a little laugh.

13

So, like I was saying, I ended up spending two years doing nothing but studying, trying to pass my exams. My father was okay with that. This was right around the time he met his second wife, so he wasn't particularly concerned about what I did. But I was starting to run out of energy. I suppose I'd just gotten really run down, that's all, but the way I saw it – well, I was thinking the same sort of things most guys tend to think when they're in that position. Here I am working my ass off to get into college just so that I can get into a company of more or less the same level as the college, and then once I get into the company I'll be swept up in the competition there . . . man, what a degrading process this is. And so on and so on.

I might not have been so good at taking exams, but I was as bright as the next guy. The thing was, though, that ultimately my talent would never be recognized as such if I kept running along the track that led from college to company. I wanted to live in a world where people weren't pigeonholed according to their academic history or what company they worked for, a world that knew how to recognize the worth of real, living people. I wanted to see what I could accomplish in a place like that. That's how I saw things then.

Between early summer and late fall of my second year, I went around looking for jobs that paid well, and working at them I managed to save up about four hundred thousand yen. I made my dad give me another five hundred thousand. I told him that I'd given up on college. That I was leaving for America.

And in the winter, I did just that. I went to Los Angeles. I was twenty years old. I enrolled in a language school, and I think it's fair to say that as far as *speaking* English was concerned, I improved at a slightly more rapid pace than most. I was offered a job at a fast food restaurant downtown, a place run by a Japanese guy. I went around to the main offices of all these buildings, collecting orders, and then at lunchtime I'd deliver the food. That was the work I did. I made more than I would have done washing dishes. Not everyone could handle a job like that just two or three months after they'd arrived in the US. I developed a sense of the area, and it took me hardly any time to remember customers' names. If I managed to crack a little joke when I was talking with some white person or black person, I felt that I'd been right, I really was better at these things than ordinary people. I gained confidence. As a nation, I thought, Japan was never able to give me this sort of confidence. I was right to come to America.

Needless to say, that mood didn't even last three months. So what if I could find my way around, so what if I could make a little joke every so often? There were plenty of Americans out there who could do the same thing better, and with a lot less trouble. No one was going to come and set me up with a desk and a secretary just because I could manage something as trivial as that.

I kept living from one day to the next. I couldn't really imagine a future for myself. And then they started rounding up all
the illegal Japanese workers. I just barely managed to escape.
Actually, I was pretty lucky with things like that. Sometimes I
got depressed thinking that, sure, maybe I was a tad better at
some things than other people and tended to be lucky in small
ways, but I had no special abilities and was never lucky in a big
way. That said, it's still better not to get nabbed.

Slightly less than a year later, I moved to San Francisco. I got
a job trying to bring Japanese customers into a badly placed
duty-free shop. I had wanted to change my way of life. It wasn't
much of a change, though. I ended up being pretty good at
drawing in customers, but there was no future in the job. I was
recruited twice, and changed stores. Sometimes I was involved
with a woman who came along with me, and it's not like I wasn't
having any fun, but when I look back now I'm astonished at
how tawdry my life was then.

Deep down, I always felt very depressed. What a miserable
life, I thought. There has to be something more.

Then this cook I knew invited me to help out with a
Japanese restaurant that was about to open in Portland. The
project was being financed jointly by him and a man who coor-
dinated imports for a chain of a stores in Japan selling
American goods to youngsters – there were a dozen or so of
them, from Sendai to Fukuoka. So the cook was going to be one
of the owners of the restaurant. He said there wouldn't be much
point in opening another Japanese restaurant in Los Angeles or
San Francisco, but up in Portland the chances of success were
still relatively high.

I was being brought on board as the manager. I told him it

struck me as awfully dangerous to have a manager on a student
visa, but he said, Look, you think anyone's going to take the
trouble to check? The salary was good too – that's what
attracted me. According to the cook, the location wasn't all that
great, so in the beginning they might need me to go stand on
the corner and try to talk Japanese tourists into coming inside,
just as I'd done for the duty-free shops. You might think that
would have discouraged me, but actually when I heard that I
felt as if I'd finally understood what they were after. So I agreed
to do it. I wasn't completely sure I was doing the right thing, but
I was pretty happy to be getting out of San Francisco.

Portland, Oregon, was a nice town – picturesque and cozy.
The cook and I were happy to find that the staff at the hotel we
stayed in at first didn't have the hard edge common to residents
of big cities.

There was one hitch, however: we weren't able get in touch
with the coordinator, who was supposed to have arrived before
us. He didn't answer when we called the telephone number he'd
given us.

We went downtown the next day to take a look at the restaurant, the interior of which was supposed to be finished already,
but when we reached the address it was a parking lot. We
walked around the block any number of times, and only then,
at long last, did we realize that we'd been tricked. The cook was
thirty-five or thirty-six, but when I heard his account of the
details of the deal, I could see he was unbelievably naive. And I
had been unbelievably innocent, going along so easily with the
plan he proposed. Sometimes when you hear about a person
who's been involved in some kind of fraud, you wonder how he
or she could ever have been taken in by something so ridicu-

lous, but the thing is – it's like magic, the way these con artists take hold of people's hearts. They can tell the ones who are easy to deceive from those who aren't.

It was a major blow for the cook. He'd sunk more than half his savings from the six years he'd been living in San Francisco into that deal. In the parking lot he tried to laugh it off – 'That's life, huh?' he said, his face pale – but later, when we went into a restaurant to have lunch, he couldn't swallow a bite. Then, after we had left the restaurant and walked a block or so, he fainted all of a sudden and hit his head hard on the pavement.

I still had a little money left. I moved to a cheaper place where the injured cook and I lived together for a couple of weeks. During that time I went out to look for a job and started washing dishes. The cook said his head hurt and did no work at all, and he was always flying into a rage, swearing he was going to go back to San Francisco and get revenge on the guy who'd tricked us. With things as they were, I couldn't just keep taking everything with a smile. Eventually the cook and I had a fight and he left.

About a month later, one good thing and a few bad things happened, all at the same time. Though to tell the truth, the good thing that happened was really pretty insignificant, and the bad things were about twenty or thirty times bigger.

It was the end of March. I was heading out of my room in that cheap hotel one evening, on my way to go wash dishes. As soon as I opened the door, two men came in, their faces perfectly calm, as if they had just walked up to an automatic door and it had slid open. They knocked me down so easily it was like they were brushing a cobweb off their faces or something, and then they kicked me in the stomach, and before I even had a chance to cry out they were stomping on my back.

By the time I came to, all my money was gone. They hadn't left me a cent. My left eye was swollen. And I could taste blood in my mouth. My back and my right leg both hurt like hell, but I figured I should count myself fortunate that I hadn't been stabbed. I staggered outside. I knew there was no point reporting what had happened to the police: it would have been a complete waste of time. I was penniless, so I didn't have the option of taking the night off. I wouldn't have been able to work if I'd been a waiter, but it would be no inconvenience to the customers if the dishwasher's face was puffy. So I started walking toward the restaurant, dragging my right leg behind me.

The reason I hadn't gotten a room in a cheap apartment out in the suburbs but instead stayed at a slightly more expensive hotel downtown was that I had no car. The buses didn't run that frequently, and they made so many twists and turns that it took a full thirty minutes for them to cover the same distance you could do in five minutes in a car. In the end, it was just more convenient for me to live in a downtown hotel if I was going to be washing dishes in a restaurant in that area.

It was right around then that the good thing happened. What happened was that I managed to escape being caught in an Immigration Bureau sweep of illegal foreign workers in Portland, just as I had in Los Angeles. I had the two men who attacked me to thank for this. When I got close to the Japanese restaurant where I'd been working, I saw a bunch of uniformed immigration officers loading everyone I'd been working with into the back of a big van.

I spun on my heel and started heading back to the hotel right away. Now I wouldn't be able to have dinner, either. Or, of course, breakfast the next morning. I'd already paid the next week's bill at the hotel, so at least I didn't have to worry about that for the next three days. There was no way I could go without eating for three days, though. And I wasn't sure whether or not I'd be able to find another job so soon after a sweep.

I'd have to try and move as little as possible. To stay asleep. That was the only thought that came to me as I walked. I returned to the hotel, tumbled into bed, and lay there with my eyes closed, not thinking of the future.

I couldn't keep doing that for ever, though. The next day I traipsed around looking for work, but just as I'd expected, every place I tried said they weren't planning to hire anyone for a while. Swallowing my pride, I went to the restaurant I'd been working at until the previous day and requested a loan of fifty dollars. I was so hungry I was getting wild. They lent me ten dollars.

* * *

It took me a while to get through the opening segment of my story. 'It was the next morning that I met Eric. It's not much of a story . . . were you listening?'

'*I certainly was. I was enthralled.*'

'You don't need to go to the bathroom?'

'*You seem to go a lot.*'

'No, I'm okay.'

'*I'm okay too.*'

'I'd like to get a sip of water, though.'

'*Go right ahead. I've got a bar of chocolate in front of me. I'll have a piece of that.*'

14

Right in the center of town there was this place called Pioneer Square. It was also known as Courthouse Square, because that's where the courthouse was. There was this one time, around dawn – I'm not sure exactly what time it was – the time of day when sleepy-looking morning light starts to spread out over the sky, ever so faintly, and the street lamps seem to be dozing, their lights still burning. I was sitting on a flight of steps over in one corner of the deserted square.

I'd been having trouble sleeping. So I would go out and wander around while it was still dark. That wasn't a good thing to be doing. It was dangerous, and there was a good chance I'd be stopped by the police. The thing was, I was suffering from a mild case of claustrophobia, and didn't like staying in the hotel room. Whenever I lay down in bed, a sense of unease would start to seethe within me, bubbling toward the surface, and before I knew it my breath was so labored I was practically gasping for air.

I sat in the square, totally worn out, feeling as if nothing mattered. At that point, the only thing anyone could have taken from me was my life, after all, and as far as I was concerned, whoever wanted it was welcome to it. I was cold. But even so, I didn't want to go back to my room.

When Eric appeared in the dimly lit square, he came from

over by the river. Not that you can see the river from the square. I mean, I'm not saying he'd come from the river or anything. Just that he appeared from that direction, toward the edge of town where the Willamette River flows, not from where the mountains are.

He was a white guy, with long legs and a slightly curved back; his hair was brown. In reality he was exactly forty years old, but judging on a Japanese scale he looked as if he was about forty-five or six. He had on a rather worn beige jacket and a long brown cashmere muffler. He kept walking toward me, his head down. Of course I only found out the muffler was cashmere later; at the time the only thing that struck me was that he didn't seem like a policeman or mugger.

Eric continued walking in my direction, cutting diagonally across the square. He didn't appear to have noticed me. He kept his eyes down and slowly walked closer and closer to me, taking big strides; he seemed to be thinking about something. And then, when he was about five meters away, without once lifting his face to look in my direction, he turned toward the mountains and walked back out of the square.

Or so I thought. According to Eric, though, he was looking at me. 'I've trained myself not to be too obvious when I stare,' he told me later, laughing.

Eric said it was like a dream, finding this Asian boy sitting there all alone at dawn in the square. 'There was something about the scene that made it difficult for me to believe it was true. You'll probably be offended by this, but I felt as if I'd happened across someone very powerless and very beautiful.'

Eric was short-sighted; I was twenty-two at the time, no longer a boy; my left eye was swollen; and I was completely worn out – not a beautiful sight at all. The one thing he was right about was that I was powerless.

Eric's footsteps had faded into the distance, but then almost immediately I heard them coming back. And that sound was all it took – I could feel sweat breaking out all over my body. Here we go again. More trouble. But I didn't have the energy to take action right away, to get up and leave the square behind. Then again, there was something in Eric's appearance that made me feel he wasn't the sort of man who would do anything too bad.

'Is anything wrong?' Eric asked me. 'I mean, I just thought I'd ask . . .'

'Nothing at all,' I replied immediately, turning around to look at him. 'Just out taking a morning walk. Everything's A-Okay. Thank you for asking.'

'Don't mention it. I was just wandering around myself. I couldn't sleep.'

Eric directed a little smile at me from where he stood about eight meters away, then walked away from me again, taking the same big steps.

'What am I saying?' I thought. 'Everything's A-Okay?' Everything's awful, I'm at the end of my rope, no? For a guy like him to come along on a morning like this and start talking to me – who knows, this might be the luckiest thing that's ever going to happen to me! And I don't grab that opportunity, I just try to look cool with an 'Everything's A-Okay'. What the hell did I say that for?

I stood up and peered in the direction Eric had gone. I couldn't see him any more. And then, all at once, I found myself overwhelmed by a sense that if I didn't act now it would be too late, there would be no turning back, and I started running. When I got around the corner, I caught sight of Eric's back: he was striding off down the gray, deserted street.

'Sorry! *Sumimasen!*'

Eric turned around. I ran over to where he stood and said, panting even though I had hardly run any distance at all: 'To tell the truth, I really am in trouble.'

* * *

I suppose it's more accurate to call them antiques, rather than just saying that they were second-hand. Eric's store dealt exclusively in old light fixtures. He didn't have that many candelabras and things like that, though – most of his stock consisted of fixtures for electric lights. The storefront was only about as wide as two tatami, but the store was very deep; he seemed to have modeled the place on old shops of the sort you might find in London or somewhere. I don't mean to suggest that it was dusty or anything, though, because it wasn't: the wallpaper was neat and clean, and the gold lettering on the front window was perfect, not flaking off at all. This total lack of any indication of age made me think of those buildings done in a nineteenth-century style that you see in Disneyland and places like that, but Eric liked the store a lot, and he took good care of it. On the second floor of the building there were two bedrooms, a living room, and a kitchen, all of which Eric had to himself.

We walked through the still-dark store and went up the stairs, and Eric showed me into the living room. He said he was going to have breakfast now and asked if I'd care to join him.

I was no longer trying to look cool. As we were walking, I

had rattled on in my poor English about how I'd been robbed and lost my job. 'If you have any work for me to do, please allow me to do it,' I'd begged.

Eric had replied, just as we arrived in front of the store, 'Let me ask you a few questions first.' We ended up having breakfast first, before the questions.

Eric scrambled four eggs in the kitchen. We also had tea and cereal with milk. Americans eat a lot of cereal. After two years I still wasn't used to that and wished I could just have some bread instead, but right then I was in no position to be picky. Eric's unexpected generosity had left me feeling rather overwhelmed, both immensely grateful and slightly humiliated.

As we were eating our breakfast, Eric started chuckling.

'Come to think of it,' he said, 'I only have one question.'

'What?' I put all I had into the smile I gave him then.

'What's your name?'

What's your name. And with that, Eric burst out into such uproarious laughter you'd think he just cracked his best joke.

'Tsu-ney-oh? Would Chuney be all right?'

'Absolutely.'

Anything would be fine, as long as he'd give me a job.

'It's great timing. A guy who worked here for two years just quit. You can stay in that bedroom over there.'

'We can have our meals together, if that's all right with you. The store is closed Saturday afternoons and all day Sunday. I have a small house in Cannon Beach, and I usually spend my weekends there. I don't really go there to be alone or anything, though, so you're more than welcome to come along if you want. Of course, you can just decide that stuff later. In the beginning your job will be to do the cleaning, laundry, and cooking. With time, you'll start to acquire some knowledge of the things I sell here. Then I'll have you take care of the store. I'll give you a raise when that happens. But since you'll be living here and getting free meals, I'll only be able to offer you this much at first.'

The weekly salary Eric wrote down for me was so exorbitant I thought he must have made some kind of mistake. Without even meaning to, I found myself asking him if he really meant it, and he confirmed that the figure was correct. Though I tried not to let it show, I was thrilled at my good luck.

* * *

Eric was a very attractive person.

Even when there were no customers in the store, he'd sit gazing in rapture at the lighting fixtures he sold, saying how marvelous they were – though as far as I could tell they were just old lamps, and terribly shiny and elaborate ones at that. He loved old-time crooners like Frank Sinatra and Tony Bennett, and if he occasionally put on some classical music it was likely to be Tchaikovsky or something. At first I wasn't sure how to respond, it's true, but these were the things that gave Eric his charm.

His fondness for Tchaikovsky ran very deep, for instance. He had an astonishing number of records with different per-formances of the same piece, and over time, as I had to listen to them, I came to realize that I had never once really *listened* to Tchaikovsky's violin concerto. After a month or so, I too came to love Tchaikovsky. The same was true of Sinatra and Bennett: when I paid attention, I could see that they were both incredible singers. Eric taught me that adults can be intoxicated by music too, and in a different way from how youngsters are when they listen to modern jazz or rock. The light fixtures I had thought at first looked so cheap were in fact an essential element in a European-style room. I realized how shallow my own tastes had been. Eric was a really wonderful teacher. After about a month and a half, I was completely taken with him. Paintings I'd seen reproduced so often in textbooks that I was sick to death of them looked as striking as they had the first time once I came to see them through his eyes. He had a peculiar talent for breathing life into things that had been passed around so much they seemed hackneyed now, like Whitman's poetry or *Rip Van Winkle*.

Of course, Eric was working most of the week, and business was pretty good, so generally I was only able to listen to him talk for about two hours every night, up in the living room. He almost always set that time aside for me, though. I suppose my eagerness made it seem worthwhile for him too, because I got the sense he was working out a plan right from the morning, every day, deciding what he would spring on me that night. I really looked forward to those talks too.

On the weekends, we would go to Cannon Beach. It took about two hours to get from the city to the beach, driving west to the Pacific shoreline. There was a huge rock out in the ocean. At low tide you could walk all the way out, and every so often when you looked in its direction you would see people climbing it. There were lots of seagulls, too.

Eric's little house was on a bluff facing the ocean, though it wasn't a very high one, and if you put a handful of potato chips on the veranda several dozen seagulls would come flapping over, so that in no time at all the chips would be gone. Then they would wait for the next distribution, hovering in the air around the veranda. It would be quite a while before they left.

The record collection Eric had in that house was absolutely amazing. He made a big deal of love songs by unknown popular singers from thirty or forty years ago, and then he had some Schumann and Brahms and so on – there was nothing contemporary. Eric hated CDs, which had only just started appearing. He said an old love song wasn't worth a dime without the scratch of the needle.

Looking back, it's clear that Eric was being extremely circumspect. Even though I'd already come to respect him quite a lot, and listened with interest to everything he said, he still allowed more than two months to pass before he gave any sign at all of what he was actually thinking.

One evening, we had opened a bottle of wine and listened to a Bing Crosby record, and eventually decided it was about time to head off to bed. 'Good night, then,' said Eric, stretching out his long arm and putting it around my shoulder. Of course, I didn't think anything at all of that. Unlike us Japanese, people in America are very casual about making that sort of bodily contact, and we'd both gotten a little drunk too, so I gave him a gentle hug in return before going off to my room. That time, though, I felt something a little different. I had the sense that the few seconds he'd hugged me had lasted just the tiniest bit longer than usual. A few moments earlier I'd been on the verge of asking him why he hadn't ever married, why he didn't have a girlfriend, but then decided not to; that

question danced for a moment through my mind then, but I
didn't get any further than that.

Three or four days later, after a night spent sipping brandy,
Eric talked about what terrible people almost all the characters
in Hitchcock's films are. A little past ten o'clock, as we started
slowly making our way toward our separate bedrooms, after
we'd switched off the lights in the living room and walked
together into the hall, Eric suddenly put his arms around me
and kissed me on the lips. It wasn't a deep kiss or anything, but
I was taken completely by surprise, and because I tried to push
his lips away with my own I actually ended up puckering them
in a way that made it seem as if I were *asking* him to kiss me.
Part of the reason I didn't struggle or flail my arms was that Eric
was hugging me so tightly – but as you might expect, it wasn't
only that. I was also grateful for all the help he'd given me, and
on top of that there was the fact that I both liked and respected
him. The kiss didn't last long. Eric backed away from me after
just a moment or two, and before I knew it he was in his room
with the door closed.

I wiped my lips with the palm of my hand, feeling as though I
were about to throw up, and then, afraid Eric might hear,
I rushed into my room, shut the door behind me, and spat out as
much saliva as I was able to into in my handkerchief. I had no
tendencies of that sort whatsoever. I loved the naked female body.

And yet that weekend, at Cannon Beach, Eric's penis did
penetrate my rectum. And that wasn't all. Whenever Eric pene-
trated me, my own penis grew hard, and every time, each and
every time, I ejaculated.

That was a terrible shock. I felt totally beaten down, like a
virgin who has just been raped, and even though I thought it

was a really pathetic response, I spent all day Sunday lying motionless in my bed.

Eric was gentle with me. He didn't say a single word to try and justify what he had done, but he made breakfast and lunch himself and brought them to my bedside. I didn't even look at him. But by dinnertime, I started to feel as if I were being too weak. I couldn't just lie there feeling beaten down for ever, so I went out and sat down at the kitchen table, wearing an ambiguous expression on my face. That wasn't the right thing to do, unless I was prepared to accept Eric's advances. I should have walked right out of the house, telling him, 'Goodbye for ever.'

On the other hand, it would have been pretty hard to leave the house, make my way to downtown Cannon Beach, and get back to Portland without a car – and above all, I wasn't prepared to part with Eric or leave behind the three months of easy living I'd enjoyed with him. I was also frightened at the thought of giving up the startlingly high salary I'd been getting to go out and wander the streets again, as I had before.

So when Eric gave a faint smile and said something to me, I'd nod without looking his way, and maybe once every three times he cracked a joke I'd twist my face into something like a grin, and in the end I did ride back to Portland in Eric's car, and on Monday morning I started the day's work by wiping down the front window.

That week, I allowed Eric to penetrate me twice. I had no idea how things would develop, and I was secretly feeling shaken and bewildered. I had run headlong from Japan, where the school one went to and the company one works for are given an inordinate importance, searching for a world where people's personal worth determines who wins or loses; it would just be too pathetic for me to arrive back at Narita Airport having become a homosexual. It's not that I have anything against homosexuals. I really did think Eric was a great guy, after all. I simply couldn't stand the thought that over time I would grow to like being kissed by bearded men and the feel of hairy legs brushing against mine. Still, despite everything, I didn't run away.

It was June then, so Eric bought me shirts and sneakers appropriate to the season. And I allowed him to give me those gifts.

I was frightened, though, even as I accepted them. I was angry with myself. What kind of man are you? Why don't you run away? I didn't have enough money to return to Japan, but I had more than enough to buy a plane ticket to Los Angeles or thereabouts. Eric was even nicer and more attractive to me than he had been before. His face looked something like the actor Donald Sutherland's, except that he didn't have that eerie aura about him that Sutherland has.

Sometimes when I was working, or when we were eating dinner, or listening to some record in the living room, I'd notice that Eric looked beautiful to me, and that observation would throw me into confusion. It struck me that if things continued as they were, I'd end up becoming a man who tended completely in that direction.

The next weekend arrived. On Saturday afternoon, we headed out to Cannon Beach again. Eric said he'd been looking forward to that weekend a lot. He told me he didn't like forcing people to do things they didn't want to do. Which meant he was

expecting me to come throw my arms around him or something on my own during the course of the weekend – to be a
little active, rather than simply put up with the things he did to
me, as though I were a wooden doll. There was no way I could
ever do that. And yet I probably would. I couldn't say for sure
about this weekend, but I felt fairly certain I'd do something the
weekend after.

The road to Cannon Beach didn't follow the shoreline. A
long stretch of it seemed to have been cut out of a forest, and
there were rows of tall evergreen trees on either side. It was a
monotonous road. The sky was overcast. The radio said it was
probably going to rain. It rained a lot in that region. If it rained,
we wouldn't be able to go out onto the beach. How would I
spend the weekend then, shut up inside with Eric? I was afraid.
It wasn't so much Eric who scared me; I was afraid of myself. I
had never even imagined a life like that, setting up a household
with another man.

I found myself wishing that some powerful force would do
me a favor and crush the life I was living. An earthquake would
do the trick. Or a fire. Or if we got into an accident right now, in
this car. Sitting there next to Eric as he drove, I was holding back
the impulse to suddenly reach over and grab the steering wheel
and drive the car into one of the trees in the forest that surrounded us.

But wishing was all that I ever did. What a wimp.

The car arrived without incident at Cannon Beach, which
was the same as always, and pulled up in front of the small
house.

Eric opened the door and I followed him in, carrying a
cardboard box full of food and beer. As I set the box down on

the kitchen table, Eric came up and hugged me from behind. I felt him kissing my neck, and then he spun me around to face him and suddenly slid his tongue between my lips. I placed a hand on his chest and pushed him back. 'I want to go to Seaside for a little,' I said. Seaside is a proper noun: it's a small town about twenty minutes from Cannon Beach by car.

'Why?' Eric said, sounding slightly displeased.

'There's something I need to buy.'

'What are you going to buy in Seaside? There's nothing there.'

'I still want to go,' I said, growing a trifle stubborn. 'I want to make a quick trip, that's all. Do I have to tell you every little thing I want to buy? I'll be back in under an hour.'

'All right.' Perhaps Eric was intimidated by the anger in my voice, because he was very quick to give in. 'I'll get dinner ready while you're out. Here, go.' He dug the car key out of his pocket and dropped it onto my palm. 'In return, though, I'd like you to leave your backpack here.'

I glanced at Eric's face, startled. My passport and my wallet were both inside my backpack. Eric looked away.

'Just take as much money as you need to do your shopping, okay? I know this sounds unpleasant, but I'm worried. Sometimes I start thinking you might go off somewhere and leave me, and I feel so bad I can hardly stand it.'

It was clear to me just how hard it was for him to say that.

'No problem,' I said. I took my wallet out of my backpack and spread out all the money I had on the table. Even the change. I half expected him to tell me I didn't need to go that far, but he just looked on in silence.

'I'll take fifty dollars, that's all.'

'Take more than that.'

'No, this is enough,' I said.

Then I hoisted my backpack up onto my shoulder and walked outside. I'm sure Eric must have wanted to ask me why I was taking the backpack, but he didn't speak. I suppose he didn't want to make me angry.

As I put the car in motion, a sense of failure came welling up inside me: my plan had been spoiled. I had managed on the spur of the moment to find a way to keep my passport, but I wouldn't be able to fly anywhere on fifty dollars, even if I did rush right to the airport.

Thinking back on everything now, I can see that, even so, I really should have returned to Portland. I could have dealt with the money situation somehow. I should have called my father and asked him to telegraph money to me, as I would later on from Los Angeles.

That's not how I saw things then, though. Instead, for the first time, I began to feel hatred for Eric. I began to think he'd been exploiting the power he had over me. Leave your money and your backpack. That, I thought, is how he's going to hold onto me, keep me from leaving him, that's how he'll play with my life, turn me into his toy. I have to do something. I don't love Eric at all, I don't even like him – no, I hate him, some-how I have to make him realize.

But I wasn't sure I was that brave. Eric was naive. My words would hurt him terribly. And all he had done was lend me a helping hand when I had nowhere left to go, and then fall in love with me. If possible, I didn't want to do anything that would hurt him too badly, no frontal blows, because he had been so nice. I wanted him to give up on me all on his own.

What if I did something really messed up, how would that be? I could do something so wild he'd no longer even be able to imagine living with me.

All I can say is that I was confused. I only meant it as a prank. Of course, Eric would be furious. The weekend would be ruined. But that's all I thought would happen, nothing more than that, and besides, at that point, destroying the atmosphere seemed like the best thing I could hope to accomplish that weekend.

There was pretty much only the one main street in Seaside, but even so there was a small movie theater, some restaurants, an arcade, and a disco, and there tended to be a fair number of people around on the weekends. Cars were parked up and down both sides of the street.

If you went just one street over from the main street, there were no stores and hardly any people. I parked the car there and called the police from a payphone.

The officer who answered sounded really tired. His tone didn't change at all when I told him that Eric Roob, in Cannon Beach, had heroin in his house. 'What, did you have a fight with this Eric Roob guy or something?' he said with a mocking laugh. Then he asked, 'Where in Cannon Beach did you say this guy lives?' I repeated the number of the house, and then, egged on by the fact that the officer didn't seem the slightest bit surprised, 'You get what I'm saying, right? This isn't a joke. The trunk of his car is filled with heroin. He and a couple of other men are dividing it up.' With that, having told my ludicrous lie, I hung up.

I went into a hamburger stand, had a Coke, and went back to the car. If my call wasn't brushed off as a prank, they'd probably send out a patrol car and the house would be searched. Eric would be made to face the wall and lift his hands in the air, and he'd probably protest, in that unique, slightly halting way of his: 'Me and a few other men? I've never heard anything so ridiculous!' Maybe he would secretly be blaming me. He was unlikely to say anything, though. And then, since there'd never been any heroin in the first place, the police would leave. I'd come back just after they left. And I'd tell Eric that I was the one who phoned them. He would fly into a rage. Then, no doubt, it would be easier for me to talk to him. To tell him I had wanted to ruin the weekend. That I simply couldn't stand being in this sort of a relationship.

* * *

I had to time my return carefully. I had no desire to meet up with the police officers and have them interrogate me. I would park the car on the public road. When you turned off the public road you drove onto a dirt road that led up to the top of the cliff, and there was nothing up there but Eric's house. If I ran into the police after I'd turned onto that road, it would be hard for me to claim I had no relationship with Eric. And if the officer who'd taken my phone call had his wits about him at all, he might well have alerted the other officers, telling them that the snitch had spoken pretty bad English and might possibly have been Japanese. If I were to show up without a care in the world in the middle of all that, I could well end up in a much worse position than Eric.

I went back to Cannon Beach with these thoughts running through my mind. As I drew near the turnoff to Eric's house on the public road, I saw a few patrol cars and a bunch of policemen climbing out of them. They were right at the corner of the dirt road leading up to the house. I drove by without stopping, looking out as I passed. There were four cars. I saw the officers starting up the dirt road toward the house.

I hadn't expected things to get so serious. But of course there had never been any heroin in the first place, and there were no other men, and no trunk, so even if Eric did end up being taken in and the whole house was searched from top to bottom, there was no need to worry about anything worse – no danger, in other words, that Eric might go to prison or anything like that. And if he was taken in, he'd still be released. I myself would be in considerable jeopardy for making a false report, to be sure, but Eric would be safe. If he ended our relationship, I thought, well, that was exactly what I wanted.

I drove on about two hundred meters and turned onto another road that led up to the top of the cliff, just like Eric's. This road was paved; there were four or five houses on either side and up at the top. I parked the car in an empty lot just around the bend and started hurrying through the tall grass toward Eric's house.

I had to tread quietly. The officers were likely to be carrying pistols with their safety catches off. If they heard me running up behind them, they were sure to open fire.

When I'd walked a few dozen meters, I got down on my hands and knees and started crawling. That didn't help with the grass, though – there was no way to avoid making it move. I had no choice but to stop at the farthest point from which I had a view of Eric's house. I found myself looking down at it from a position about five or six meters away and slightly uphill, hiding myself in the grass.

Eric's house was utterly still.

Were the officers already inside? Dusk was overtaking the cloudy sky.

There was a light on in the living room, which looked out over the ocean. There was also a light on in the kitchen.

Then someone moved outside. I saw two officers going quickly along the side of the house, crouched down, heading around to the back. It seemed like a pretty exaggerated response, but then on the other hand, if they had taken my story about the trunk full of heroin and the other men seriously, I guess it was only normal.

After that, two more officers started coming up the road. They headed straight for the front door. One of them was carrying a small axe. What are they doing, I thought, are they planning to break down the door? But that's ridiculous! There's no need to do that, Eric will open the door!

The man in front was short and plump; the second guy, who had the axe, was tall. The shorter of the two turned his head this way and that, as if he were looking for the doorbell. There was no doorbell. He would have to knock. He knocked. There was no response. He knocked again. Hurry up and answer the door, Eric! If you don't hurry these guys are going to break down the door with that axe! Still there was no response. He had to be able to hear that knocking, whether he was in the kitchen or the living room.

I could hear the crashing of the waves, but it wasn't loud enough to drown out those knocks. The short officer tried knocking a bit longer this time. The more he knocked, the more force he used. Then suddenly he drew back.

Before I even knew what was happening, the tall officer had

swung the axe down into the door, hitting it close to the lock.
There was an awful splintering sound. He took another swing.
Just then, I heard Eric's voice. He was outside.

'What are you doing?'

There was an iron ladder that went down the cliff to the
beach. Eric had shouted up at the officers from the ladder, as he
climbed up. *What are you doing?*

He had shouted at almost the exact moment he reached the
top of the ladder and hoisted himself to a standing position on
the cliff. And just then, at almost the same moment, there was
another sound. The sound of a pistol firing.

It wasn't either of the men at the front door. It was another
officer, positioned somewhere outside my field of view.

All of a sudden, Eric was gone.

'Who just fired?' shouted the short officer at the front door,
crouching down.

The man with the axe was almost flat on his stomach.

After that, no one moved.

I heard the crashing of the waves. And the cries of seagulls.

It would have been a nice, quiet evening, if only I could forget what had just taken place between Eric and the police. I
wanted to forget.

What had happened to Eric? Maybe the bullet had only
grazed him? Maybe he had only ducked down because he was
so surprised?

Hearing something by the front door, I looked over and saw
the two officers, the short one and the tall one, posing theatri-
cally on either side of the door and diving into the house. Two
more officers sprinted into view right away and ran in after
them, crouching down close to the ground.

Another two officers started heading over toward Eric, keeping their pistols pointed in his direction. They moved very slowly, holding their guns out in front of them at just the same height.

I kept waiting for Eric to stand up, raising his hands over his head. But he didn't get up, even when the officers arrived at the spot where he lay. I wanted to see him lying there, but the grass was too high.

One of the officers bent down beside him; the other just lowered his gun and stood there looking down.

'Is he okay?' I heard a voice at the front door. It was the short officer.

The officer standing by Eric turned to look at the short officer and shook his head. The short officer cursed quietly and spat on the porch.

Eric was dead.

15

I ran to the car and drove straight back to Portland. It occurred to me that the police might think it strange if they found Eric's car back in the city, but I had no idea whether or not there was a bus then, and while I might be able to flag down the Gray Line Coast Tour the next day. I only had fifty dollars on me. It didn't seem like a good idea to spend the night on Cannon Beach either because the police might start searching it. So I had no choice but to take Eric's car. I had no choice really, I kept saying, berating myself in an effort to suppress the panic I felt.

After I'd driven for twenty minutes, it started to rain. Night had fallen.

The rain was fierce but intermittent. One moment it would be falling so hard I felt as if it were aimed specifically at me, then suddenly it would slack off and turn into a shower, and then once more, in the blink of an eye, it would start pouring so hard the wipers could hardly manage to keep up.

And my emotions were every bit as variable as the rain. Calm down. You may have avoided him, but that won't help you if you get in an accident.

If I managed things very carefully, there was still a good chance I might be able to salvage my life. I couldn't afford to panic. Eric's death was an accident. I can't let myself feel overly responsible for what happened and get desperate. I was defending my way of life. Think about what to do now. About how to get out of this situation.

It was past eight when I drove into Portland. I had been very careful not to drive too fast, so the trip had taken a full two hours. Though of course, the quicker I acted the better.

I steered clear of the lot where Eric always left his car, parking instead on the street, a little way off. After all, I couldn't be sure the police in Cannon Beach hadn't contacted the officers here, and that they weren't waiting there in the lot for me now. I was taking a gamble – that's what it felt like. I had no choice but to. Everything would be all right if I could just make it to Los Angeles. If only I had enough money to live for a few days in Los Angeles once I'd made it there . . . That's what I was thinking.

I got my set of keys out of my backpack and made my way through the rain toward Eric's shop. When I was a block away, I quickly scanned the area around the store. There was no sign of anyone. The rain was pouring down hard, so I didn't have the luxury of being any more cautious than that. If the police had surrounded the place, I'd just have to deal with it. It wasn't as if I were sneaking into someone else's house. I lived there. Besides, I wasn't the one who killed Eric. Some cowardly officer had opened fire, startled by the unexpected shout. It was a murder that never should have happened. Who in their right mind would ever make a prank call if they knew it would lead to something like that?

I raised the security shutter and went in. The interior of the shop, which Eric had loved so much, was dimly illuminated by the rain-wet street lights outside; it looked the same as always,

as if nothing had happened. At least, that's the impression I
have when I think back on that night now – at the time I didn't
have the luxury of taking a little break to stand there, looking
the place over. I went right up to the second floor and dug out
the change purse I'd hidden under my bed, in the toe of one of
my boots. There was a hundred dollars in it. It was my money.
I'd put it aside in case of an emergency.

After that, I searched the living room and Eric's bedroom
for cash. I remembered Eric telling me that he always left some
money around. If a burglar should ever break in, he said, it
would be better to have him go away feeling at least a little sat-
isfied, rather than to have him find nothing at all and take out
his anger by smashing everything in the store. I sensed from
the way he said this that he was only telling me because he
knew 'his Chuney' (Tsuneo) wasn't the sort of person to take
the money, and so I'd never even wondered where he might
have put it. And here I was, frantically hunting for it, as if it
were my only hope. There was a broken Rolex in Eric's desk,
but I suspected it would be hard to get money for it. I put it in
my pocket anyway, though, just in case. I found a hundred
dollars under the penholder in the living room and another
hundred under the ashtray in the bedroom. (Eric had given up
smoking ages ago, but he treasured that big ashtray, which he
said he'd bought in Sorrento, Italy.) The hiding places were so
artlessly chosen I could hardly believe it. And two hundred
dollars was too much money just to leave lying around like
that. Could it be, I wondered, that this had been yet another
expression of his faith in me? Betraying his trust, I took the
money, packed all my things in Eric's traveling bag, and went
back out the front door of the store.

I wasn't particularly attached to the things I had, and I didn't have all that many things anyway, but I wanted to leave as little trace of my presence as possible. Eric didn't have many friends, and he'd avoided introducing me to the few he did have. In part this was because I didn't want him to, because I was afraid the Immigration Bureau might find out about me somehow, but to some extent he might also have wanted to conceal the fact that he was living with a member of the 'yellow race'. No . . . no, I have no right to speak so badly of Eric.

I left Eric's car in the parking lot he always used and got a room at a cheap hotel in another part of town. I left Portland on an early flight the next morning.

* * *

'And that's all there is. That's the end of my story,' said Tsuneo. 'I came back to Japan and tried to become as ordinary and unremarkable as possible.'

'*What kind of work do you do now?*' asked the woman. Tsuneo felt as though ages had passed since he'd last heard her voice.

'I'm a civil servant. At the national level.'

'*I think I understand.*'

'Understand what?'

'*Why you were able to hear my voice —*'

'Now it's your turn.'

'*What?*'

'It's your turn to talk.'

'*No, that's all right.*'

'Why? You wanted to talk, so you poured your heart out, calling for someone. Isn't that right? I'm happy to listen, as much as you want.'

'*At the duty-free shop –*'

'The duty-free shop?'

'*You were good at bringing in customers, right? And hearing about you and Eric . . . I guess you must be a very good-looking man.*'

'You're changing the subject.'

'*My own story –*'

'Yes, your story?'

The woman fell silent.

'Of course,' said Tsuneo, 'I'll be happy to listen tomorrow when we meet under the clock at Mullion. You have to understand that what I've just finished telling you is something I have kept silent about for a long time, you know? I'm feeling excited. I really want to hear your story.'

The woman remained silent.

Then a deep emotion took hold of him. He didn't know how to express it. At first it was very faint, like the sound of the wind blowing in the distance.

'Why won't you say anything?' asked Tsuneo.

The woman didn't respond.

What he had taken at first for the rushing of wind could also have been sobbing. After a time, the voice in the distance spun around and began heading in Tsuneo's direction, swinging closer and closer.

It was screaming. The wind tore through the air like a scream. And all at once, Tsuneo was inside that wind. He clenched his hands and bit his lip, struggling to keep from being blown away. What's happening? What is this? He was being buffeted by the wind, and yet his eyes were wide open – he could see his room in the dorm, it was really there, looking just as it always did. Except that everything seemed very far away, insubstantial, unreliable, as if he were looking at a photograph, not the real thing. The wind carried an infinite number of tiny grains of sand that rained down on his skin, striking him violently. He couldn't move. He couldn't speak. What are you doing? What the hell is this woman trying to do to me? What is she trying to tell me?

The wind swept off into the distance. Unable to move, Tsuneo watched it go.

The next thing he knew, he was immersed once more in a deep emotion. A deep emotion – it was a rather vague expression, but he couldn't think how else to say it. He realized then that he was submerged in an emotion more intense than any he had ever felt before. It seemed to him that this feeling included each and every emotion that could be felt, and moreover that each individual emotion was especially dense and profound. It was quiet. He was sunk in a swamp whose surface was as still as oil. A deep, thick, dark quagmire of emotions. Like a pool into which every color had been mixed ever so persistently; all the emotions in existence had been gathered there, and no matter how hard he tried to feel any particular one – only anger, for instance, or only joy – he knew it would be impossible. Then, quietly, the swamp drew back, leaving Tsuneo behind. The barest trace of an emotion lingered in him, but that emotion was his own. It seemed a dingy, trite, and mundane thing.

16

Tsuneo arrived at Mullion at five minutes to three the next day.

Mullion was a new building in Yūrakuchō that housed two department stores and five movie theaters. With so much within its walls, it couldn't help becoming one of the centers of the bustling district in which it was located, but because there was nothing really unhealthy about it – nothing linked to the darker side of pleasure – it had a sterile feel to it. It was flavorless, lacking in depth.

Their appointment was for three-thirty. He went first and stood under the clock on the outside wall of the building, but since he still had another thirty-five minutes or so to wait he decided to go into one of the department stores.

He felt rather frightened at the prospect of finally meeting the woman, and at the same time somewhat dejected. The thought that she had succeeded in sending her voice to him, that her emotions were so powerful, repelled him somewhat, but he had also been picturing her as someone wonderfully mysterious. He suspected that no matter what sort of woman appeared, the actual sight of her there, in the flesh, was bound to prove a disappointment. But he still had to meet her. He had to confirm that she wasn't simply an auditory hallucination. Unless he was able to feel sure of that, his life would gradually fall to pieces.

He had come wearing a light-blue jacket, slightly darker pants, and a striped shirt. Once he arrived, though, he began to feel it might be better to wear a tie, so he bought one for three thousand yen in the store and put it on. But then, when he went into the bathroom and looked at himself once more in the mirror, he started to think it was kind of tacky, so he took it off and stuffed it into his pocket. He spent a while doing things like that, and then, at three-twenty, he went out and sauntered over toward the area beneath the clock once more.

The space directly beneath the clock was an entranceway, so no one was standing there. He estimated that there were about fifteen people waiting for their friends on the perimeter of that space, where it was possible to see the face of the clock. Seven or eight of them were women. Only about four of them looked as though they might be twenty-five or twenty-six. He scanned the crowd, making it clear that he was looking for someone, but no one responded to his gaze. I'll never know her. She'll have to speak to me, otherwise I'm not going to recognize her. Then it struck him: Come to think of it, she won't recognize me either.

'Hello?' Tsuneo called to the woman in his heart. 'Are you here? Hello?'

'*Yes.*'

'Oh good. Which one are you? I'm wearing a blue jacket, and I'm not carrying anything. I'll put my hand on my belt now.'

There was no response.

'Hello? Which one are you? No one even seems to be looking for me. Could you give me a sign, please? I looked for someone around twenty-five; maybe I need to expand the search a little?'

'*No.*'

'Well then, which one are you? It wouldn't surprise me to learn that you're any of these women. Everyone looks sort of lonely, come to think of it – oh, hold on. One of them is going. A man came and met her. She looks very happy. The man isn't smiling, though. He's looking away from her.'

'*I'm sorry.*'

'What?'

'*I'm not there.*'

'Where are you?'

'*By the fountain in Hibiya Park.*'

'Why there?'

'*I'm sorry.*'

'No problem,' Tsuneo said, starting to walk. 'I can be there in three minutes.'

Seeing that the green light over the crossing was flashing, he sprinted and only just made it across in time. He hurried on toward Hibiya Park. It's only natural for her to hesitate like this. I was feeling pretty nervous myself. Maybe it's better to go through some stuff like this first, rather than just meet each other all of a sudden, with no prelude or anything. Still, self-centered behavior like this is a little annoying. It was the same last night. If she didn't want to talk about herself, she could have just said so. What was she thinking, sending some whacked-out sort of wind at me, without any warning, throwing up a smokescreen?

He dashed across another crossing in front of the Imperial Hotel, toward the park. He wasn't sure he understood this woman. How could she be so nonchalant when she was making him run around like this?

He entered the wide open space where the fountain was and quickly scanned the area around the circular stone basin, but he didn't see any women who looked suitable. There seemed to be a lot of old men. The only woman he saw was a white woman sitting down on the edge of the fountain with a baby carriage beside her. A white woman? It wasn't entirely impossible, was it? She may have felt his gaze, because she lifted her face to look at him. She was rather large. 'That's not you, is it?' he said with his eyes, briefly returning her look. The woman hurriedly looked away, evidently displeased.

'Hello? I'm here now.'

There were no other women, not a single one, even on the benches near by.

'*It's a long way,*' said the woman suddenly, '*but can you walk over toward Sakurada Gate?*'

'What is this? Don't you think you're being kind of rude?'

'*The thought of meeting you scares me.*'

'I'm a little hesitant myself, but this sort of thing is childish.' Even as he said this, he was starting to walk toward Sakurada Gate. 'I don't know the details, but I understand that you're not constantly meeting a lot of people. And I assume there's a reason for that. I won't be surprised, no matter what the reason is. I asked you to meet me. I'm prepared to accept the consequences. I hope we can be together like this from now on, for ever. Not just as voices – I want to meet you and talk with you in person, build up a relationship . . .'

'*Stop –*' said the woman's voice. '*Stop right there.*'

Tsuneo was just leaving a nicely landscaped area where a

bench-lined walkway snaked between a group of low bushes. From here, all he would have in front of him was the path that led to the gate.

'*There are tennis courts up ahead, on the left.*'

'Right.'

'*I'm watching tennis there.*'

'Okay.'

He started walking forward very slowly, feeling weak at the knees. He saw the woman right away.

There were two tennis courts, separated from the walkway by a tall fence. The woman was standing alone by the fence, watching the tennis players.

Judging from her profile, and from this distance, she looked as if she were under twenty-five years old. She had short hair. She was wearing a floral-patterned dress, and had a yellow summer cardigan draped over her shoulders. No, no – it wasn't draped over her shoulders, she was wearing it. A red handbag hung from her arm. Her high heels were red too. She looked a bit like she'd come from the country.

'*Will you do me a favor?*' asked the woman with the voice, in a whisper. '*I've always wanted to have someone try to pick me up. Will you do that for me?*'

'All right.'

She looks like an ordinary person, doesn't she? Why does she feel so alone? I wouldn't say she's especially beautiful, but she looks young, and she's got nice legs.

'*Please,*' said the woman. '*Pretend we don't know each other.*'

'All right.'

In San Francisco, in the area around Union Square, he'd had to go out and strike up conversations with women tourists every day. But that was work. Sometimes he had ended up hitting on them, or doing something close to that, but he'd never done that in Japan.

Here goes, then. Think of it as a game.

He went and stood beside the woman and watched the tennis players. Two men were playing.

'Do you like tennis?' asked Tsuneo, smiling.

'Yes,' replied the woman, without putting up her guard at all.

'Don't you think . . .' he said in his heart to the woman. 'I don't know, wouldn't it be better to say something that makes it clear who you are?'

'*Good point.*' The woman gave a dry laugh.

'I used to play too, but it's so expensive in Tokyo, and who has the time?'

'You're so right,' said the woman, following the ball with her eyes.

'I wonder who these men are? To be able to play on these courts?'

'Oh!' The woman shied away. The ball had struck the fence in front of her.

'God, they suck!' grumbled Tsuneo.

'Shh,' hissed the woman, giving a little titter, afraid the man who had come to get the ball might hear.

How can this be? Can a young woman like her really be so desperately lonely that she succeeded in transmitting her voice to me? Is she just playing a role, acting with all her might like an ordinary young woman?

'Would you like to go get a cup of coffee?'

'Really? You mean that?'

'If we head back in a little, there's a coffee shop in the park.

Or we could walk out toward Ginza.'

'I feel like walking.'

'Then we'll walk.'

No sooner had Tsuneo started heading toward the intersection at Hibiya than the woman was walking alongside
him.

'I feel odd having to say this,' said Tsuneo, 'but you still
haven't told me your name.'

'My name?' The woman seemed puzzled.

'I'd like to know it.'

'Suzuki. But, I mean, is that how it goes?'

'Huh?'

'Do guys usually ask a woman's name like that? Right in the
beginning?'

'I don't know what guys usually do. I just wanted to know.
What's your given name? Suzuki what?'

'Reiko.'

'Written with the character for "lovely," I assume?'

'Yow!' The woman pretended to stumble clumsily, as if she
had been bowled over. 'That hurts!'

She laughed.

Tsuneo's face went pale. 'Where are you?' he said in his
heart. 'This isn't you. This woman isn't you.'

'To tell the truth, I don't know Tokyo very well.'

The other woman, Reiko, kept talking. The woman with the
voice didn't reply.

'I'm sorry,' Tsuneo told Reiko. 'You don't know me, do you?'

'What are you talking about?'

'Do you know the haiku that begins "Turn to face this
way"?' In his agitation, he had asked a stupid question.

'A haiku?'

'I'm really sorry. Something has come up. I can't go with you after all. Sorry.'

He was still speaking as he ran off toward the tennis courts.

The woman with the voice was watching us. She has to be somewhere near by. What the hell is she doing? She drags me out here like this, then shoves me off on some random woman. I can't believe it.

There hadn't been anyone else by the tennis courts. And yet clearly she had to have been somewhere where she could see Tsuneo standing by the fence. There was no sign of anyone around now, either.

Just then, someone moved behind one of the bushes over toward Sakurada Gate. In a flash, Tsuneo started running. But then, almost immediately, he realized that there was a public toilet back there. He'd seen someone coming out. Tsuneo was on the verge of stopping in his tracks when he noticed something: the person who'd emerged from the restroom was a small, middle-aged woman in a gray jacket. He was thunderstruck. The woman was carrying a blue plastic bucket. She must be a cleaning woman who works in the park. Something in her fair-skinned profile sent a shiver down Tsuneo's spine. Some sort of instinct told him this was her. The woman started trudging down a narrow path that led toward Shinbashi; evidently she hadn't even noticed that Tsuneo was there. She told me she was twenty-five! She's at least forty-five though, maybe forty-six. I can see why she didn't want to meet me. There was no mistaking the sense of loneliness that hung over her back as she walked away. I get it now. That's the kind of person she is. Why didn't she just say so? Did she think I'd laugh at her or something? I might not be able to fall in love with her or anything like that, but I'm perfectly happy to be friendly with her. Tsuneo followed the woman at a distance of five or six meters. She had on sneakers and a pair of gray pants that looked as if they had been washed dozens of times. The thought that such a small, serene-looking person could harbor a raging, sensuous storm like the one he had felt inspired a sort of sadness in him. He felt as if he could understand where that current of sadness had come from. If she wanted him to, he would be willing to respond to her desires.

Tsuneo called out to the woman. 'There's nothing to be afraid of.'

She kept walking, as if she hadn't heard. Tsuneo dashed around in front of her and blocked her way. 'Everything would have been fine,' he said, 'if you had just been honest with me from the beginning.'

Fear showed in the woman's eyes.

'It's you, right?'

Suddenly Tsuneo began to feel less sure of himself. As he took a step forward, the woman backed away, her body trembling slightly, stiffening.

'It's you, isn't it?'

Am I wrong? Without even realizing what he was doing, he peered into her eyes, hoping that it was her.

'Help!' the woman screamed. Her voice was deeper and gruffer than he had expected. 'Somebody, help!' Hurling the bucket she was carrying at Tsuneo, she called out once more in her raspy voice: 'Somebody!'

'No!' Tsuneo shook his hand back and forth. 'It's not that at all! I didn't mean anything like that!'

He heard someone running toward him from behind. He started to spin around, only to have a bamboo broom come flying at him.

'No, no, it's all a misunderstanding!'

A large man crashed up against Tsuneo, then kicked him in the shins. Before he knew what was happening he had crouched down, and powerful blows were raining down on his head.

'It's a misunderstanding!' Tsuneo cried out, but the man wouldn't relent. 'You bastard, you bastard!' The man kept hitting him with all his might, hardly seeming to care where his blows landed. Tsuneo swooned for a moment, and fell.

'Stand up!' bellowed the man. 'What do you think you're doing, you bastard! And in broad daylight! I'm taking you to the cops! Stand up!'

Tsuneo couldn't very well resist by hitting back, and this man didn't seem like the sort who would listen even if he tried to explain.

'On your feet!'

'Okay, okay . . .'

Tsuneo put both hands on the ground, intentionally bending down on all fours, and gave his head a shake.

'My, did he give me a scare!' said the woman in her gruff voice.

'This part of the park – it's a blind spot,' said the man, glaring down at Tsuneo. 'Some nerve, this guy has.'

Suddenly Tsuneo made a dash for it.

He heard the two of them gasp.

An instant later they shouted. 'Hey!' 'Stop!' Tsuneo kept running. People were looking at him, but he didn't care: he

made a beeline out of the park to the Hibiya intersection and
dashed across the street toward the moat, because the signal on
that side was green.

17

'It's impossible for me to go on feeling kindly disposed toward you now. To hesitate that much is just plain selfish. You're completely wrapped up in your own emotions. You don't give the slightest thought to what I'm going through. Are you listening?'

'*Yes.*'

'I'm sick of this – I don't want to have anything more to do with you. I wanted to be nice to you, but there are limits to how much I can do when you're not willing to accept what I'm offering. I think I opened my heart up to you quite enough. I confessed things to you that I've never told anyone else. And what did you do in return? You didn't open your heart to me. You tell me you'll meet me, then you trick me. And the way you made fun of me – that was really something.'

'*You think I made fun of you?*'

'What the hell were you doing if you weren't making fun of me? What need was there for you to do what you did?'

'*It was . . .*'

'For you to hesitate that much – you were just being childish, there are no two ways about it. You're so sorry for yourself it makes me sick. Where are you now? I'm right by Wadakura

Gate. In front of the moat. It's up to you whether you want to come here or not.'

'*I'll come.*'

'Well, get a move on. I don't really feel like being kept waiting for another ten or twenty minutes.'

'*I'll come.*'

'Make it quick!'

Shouting these words in his heart, Tsuneo glanced over toward Hibiya. Evidently that was where the woman was. She would probably come down the sidewalk by the moat, then – the same one he himself had just sprinted along. There was no one there now. He peered off into the distance, waiting to see a woman appear, coming toward him from Hibiya.

Traffic was heavy on the road by where he was standing, but there was no one on the sidewalk. What the hell is she doing? I told her to come right away.

A few swans may have been swimming in the moat. The new leaves on the trees lining the sidewalk may have been swaying in the breeze. His eyes didn't take in any of that. He kept looking down the sidewalk. Finally, someone appeared there, way off in the distance. It was a woman. Is that her? She seems to be wearing a suit. She's coming this way. She's walking along at a brisk pace. She's holding some sort of briefcase or something. I can see her face, her fair skin. What does she look like? But the way she's walking – she looks like someone on a work errand. Maybe it's not her. Why can't I make out her face, though? She's coming closer and closer. I ought to be able to see her more clearly with each passing moment. And yet her face still looks just as blurry as it did at first. This is weird, he thought, and rubbed his eyes, and then, when he tried once

more to look down the sidewalk, everything went black. What
has that damned woman done to me?

'*I'm right behind you.*'

He turned his head, but he couldn't see a thing. He couldn't
move.

'Why are you doing this?'

The woman's hand grabbed Tsuneo's right arm.

'*I'm here.*'

'But I can't see you.'

'*But I'm here. I'm holding your hand.*'

Another hand, different from the one on his arm, twined
itself around his.

'Why won't you let me see you?'

'*Because you aren't strong enough to bear it.*'

'I'm not a child.'

Tsuneo shook his head, trying to free himself from the
darkness.

'*Last night, I opened my heart to you.*'

'I didn't hear you say anything.'

'*All the same, I opened my heart to you.*'

'A wind was blowing, and I felt something, but it made
no sense.'

'*That's right. This world is far removed from all you know.*'

'What are you trying to say? Talk so I can understand.'

'*That's the most I can do. That's my heart. I can't explain it any
more clearly.*'

'Whatever. Enjoy your self-love.'

'*You can't imagine how ugly I am.*'

'You're the one who refuses to show me.'

'*I can sense it. You can't imagine what I look like, or what I'm like inside – not from where you are, in your bright, happy world.'*

'Just what is it about me that strikes you as bright? Or in that story about Eric?'

'It seems bright to me.'

'Are you insulting me?'

'No, I envy you.'

'Open these eyes. Open my eyes! Help me! Is anyone there?'

'Stop, please. I'll go.'

'Don't ever come back!'

'I'll never try to talk to you again.'

'I should hope not!'

'Only –'

'I don't want to hear your conditions.'

'Let me talk to you just once more, in six months' time.'

'I don't need any more of your selfish demands.'

'I won't be able to keep up my strength unless we can agree on this.'

'What have you done to my eyes?'

Tsuneo shook off the woman's hands. She let go without resisting.

'Open my eyes!' Without even meaning to, Tsuneo found himself shouting at his invisible partner. 'Don't just leave me like this!'

'There's a whole world that you can't see.'

'Don't preach at me. What is there that I can't see?'

He rubbed his eyes. He shook his head. Darkness.

'Hey! Where are you?'

Tsuneo spread his arms wide, trying to catch the hands he'd just shaken off.

Then someone grabbed his arms. Tsuneo hurriedly grasped

the arms that had seized his; then he saw the face of a young police officer, just inches from his own. 'Oh!' He let out a startled gasp.

'What happened?' asked the young officer, his face expressionless, as he pried Tsuneo's hands from his arms.

'Just now,' said Tsuneo, 'was there a woman here?'

'She ran off.'

'Where?'

'What happened?'

'Tell me where she went!'

'That way.' The officer nodded toward Tokyo Station.

Tsuneo dashed immediately toward the crossing. But the signal was red. He let his gaze speed on ahead to where his body couldn't. He couldn't see anyone who looked like a woman, though. He stood there, so frustrated he wanted to stamp his feet.

The young police officer walked over.

'What happened?'

'You saw her, right? You saw the woman!'

'Yes —'

'What was she like?'

'What's your relationship to her?'

'I'm asking you what she looked like!'

'Oh, ordinary —'

'Ordinary? What does that mean? What point is there saying something like that? You're a police officer, aren't you?'

A look of unease showed in the officer's eyes; he seemed intimidated by the fierce expression on Tsuneo's face. 'The light's green,' he said.

'Ordinary! What the hell kind of a thing is that to say?'

He was still speaking these words when, overwhelmed by a sense of urgency, he starting running toward Tokyo Station. He didn't see any woman who looked like she could be her. And what exactly did she look like anyway? An unimaginably ugly woman, she had said, but the officer had said she was ordinary. She looked ordinary. Damn her and her exaggerations. But either way, she exists. The officer saw her. She's not just a hallucination.

* * *

The woman didn't appear again.

18

There was a lot of rain that summer.

One day in early August, around dusk, Shibata Yoshie ran into Tsuneo in the part of Shinjuku known as Kabukichō. It was the first time she had seen him since the day their engagement fell apart.

It was raining that day, too. She had been walking toward Koma Stadium when she caught sight of him, striding vigorously in her direction; he was wearing a green polo shirt and held a cheap white plastic umbrella. Oh no, she thought, what am I going to do . . . but when she murmured a tentative hello as they passed in the street, Tsuneo spun around and said, 'Hey!' A nostalgic glow spread across his face.

'Put on some weight, haven't you?' asked Yoshie.

'Hmm. No chance of that, I'm afraid. I've been way too busy.' He gave a little laugh. 'Looking pretty stunning yourself, huh?' he went on, taking a step back and eyeing Yoshie's kimono in a slightly exaggerated, teasing way. 'All dressed up!' Yoshie was rather taken aback, and found herself wondering if he'd been the sort of man who acted like this before.

'I hear you're feeling better,' she said.

To which Tsuneo replied, 'Yes, I am. I really did cause you a lot of trouble back then, didn't I? I'm back to normal now, though.' Worried that he might block the stream of people around him, he stepped to the side of the street.

Yoshie moved with him. She still had some time to spare, so she asked if he was just out having a good time.

'No, no, I'm here on business,' he replied, bursting into laughter. 'Kabukichō isn't the sort of place I feel like coming to for a good time.'

'You're busy, then?'

'Yeah, more and more Korean bars are opening, and there are incredible numbers of Filipinos coming in. I'd say the Malaysians and the Indonesians are about the only ones whose numbers have decreased. I have to work like a dog, you know, day after day. How about you? You're not working here now, are you?'

'What a thing to say! I'm on my way to Koma Stadium.'

'Ah, I see. Mori Shin'ichi?'

'Wow, that's some memory you've got!'

'You wear a kimono to go see him?'

'Of course not! Besides, he's not performing. It's *Peter Pan*.'

'Oh.'

'I'm meeting my fiancé.'

'Hey! You're engaged!'

'Everyone was having so much fun comforting me after you and I broke up that I couldn't take it, so I kind of rushed into it.'

'It's great news though, huh?'

'He's going to be taking over a small bar from his dad, in Sakuragichō.'

'Beats being in Immigration.'

'He's got four apartments. His parents do, anyway.'

'Wow. Lucky for you that we broke up then, huh?'

'Please don't say that. You'll make me feel miserable.'

'Why? You're a good person. I want you to be happy.'

'You don't mean that.'

'Listen, I'm glad I ran into you. It's wonderful news. Congratulations.'

And with that, they parted.

I guess when people get dumped they have to try and act as if everything is going just perfectly, thought Yoshie, otherwise their pride is hurt. He was a bit too bouncy, though, so it was obvious he was pretending.

* * *

Despite everything, Tsuneo worked hard all summer.

One day, Director-General Saitō passed him as he was dashing up the stairs in the office, and was so impressed by his energy that he blurted out, 'Going all out, aren't you?'

'I'm back to normal,' Tsuneo shouted back.

By then his footsteps were already moving down the hall on the third floor.

* * *

By the end of September, however, when Emoto came to visit Tsuneo at his dorm, his spirits were down again.

'I hear you've been home for a week now,' Emoto said, looking down at Tsuneo lying in his bed.

'Yeah.' Tsuneo gave a thin smile. He was unshaven, starting to grow a beard.

'They say these emotional sicknesses are worst between seasons. I assume you're taking your medicine?'

As Emoto set out the two boxed shūmai dinners he'd brought on the low table, he ran his gaze around the unkempt room. Earlier, when he called to say he'd be stopping by later in the evening, Tsuneo had told him he wanted a boxed meal from the station in Yokohama.

'I haven't been shopping lately,' Tsuneo said now, 'so I don't have anything to offer you.' Nonetheless, he stood up and took two beers from the fridge. 'You'll have to make do with this and the boxed dinner.'

'You want to go somewhere?'

'Too much of a pain to get dressed.'

'You'll just keep sinking deeper and deeper if you talk that way.'

They opened their dinners and drank their beers.

'Did anything else happen?' asked Emoto. 'Like that story you told me? About what happened in the graveyard?'

'Nothing. Nothing at all.' Tsuneo's tone sounded disappointed.

'Well, that's good news, isn't it?'

'I'm not sure you'll understand.'

'Understand what?'

'The thing is, I just feel so *flimsy*.'

'Flimsy?'

'I suffer as much as most people, I'm happy as much as most people, and I cry as much as most people. But it all feels so *flimsy* to me, seriously.'

'I kind of know what you mean.'

'Say we go on a raid and arrest some Filipino woman. As we're bringing her in, I think about how terribly she must be missing her parents and her little sisters and brothers, and about how badly she wants more money, desires it from the bottom of her heart, and I start feeling that I don't have anything like that – emotions that are so real and strong and deep. There's nothing like that inside me.'

'There's got to be something, right?'

'We lock up these Bangladeshi guys. There's no way I could even come close to feeling what they must feel when they think of the land where they were born, or about the lives they're living.'

'You're kidding yourself. Sure, they've had a hell of a hard time compared to you and me, so they may see more of the dark side of people than we do. But they're not thinking about things the way you just said, not at all. Many of them have no desire whatsoever to go back to where they were born, and there are plenty of them who are cunning and greedy and have dirty minds and are just all-round creeps. You know that, right? I'm telling you, they're not all that different from us.'

'You think something's funny and you laugh. But as you're laughing you realize that this isn't how it should be, not if you really *feel* that something's funny. You get mad. But then you realize that what you're feeling is nothing like real anger. You have a craving for something, you feel sad, but no – this isn't what it feels like when something *really* tastes good, when you're *really* sad . . .'

'Well then, what's it like?'

'What?'

'What does it *really* feel like?'

'I don't know.'

'The fact that you're thinking these things, even though you can't say how it *really* ought to feel, proves that you're kidding yourself.'

'Someone else's feelings came into me.'

'What are you talking about?'

'The sadness enters me. I feel incredibly sad. I don't have any idea where the sadness comes from. Because I'm not the one who's sad. I just feel an unbelievably deep sadness. And then, after a while, the sadness goes away. It slips away from me and it's gone. And I'm left there with nothing but my own feelings. They're so weak and pathetic I hardly feel justified in calling them feelings at all, and I start to wonder if maybe the truth is that I've never *really* been sad, not once, in my whole life. I told you about what happened in the graveyard, right? Well, I've never felt as good as I did then. Never.'

'It was *your* pants that were soiled, right? That was *your* experience.'

'But the feeling was actually someone else's.'

'Who? Whose feeling was it?'

'Someone else's feeling passed through me.'

'You expect me to believe that?'

'It's unbelievable, I know. But that's the truth. Her feelings are so deep I can't imagine getting to the bottom of them – it's just as the woman says.'

'What woman?'

'It's not the kind of thing I can explain easily.'

'There's a woman involved?'

'A thick, deep feeling passes through me. It goes right through me. And all I'm left with afterwards is my own worth-less, flimsy emotions.'

'Let's talk specifics. What about you is worthless?'

'I don't know. I'm so worthless and flimsy I don't even know.'

'What the hell are you saying?'

'I have a sense of fairness. And I know when I've done something wrong. I've tried to be a solid, upright person. But none of that is worth anything. You know, there's just nothing you can do – it's all over when something like that goes through your body. No matter what I do, no matter what I feel, I know it's not *really* like this. Like an idiot I try to be normal, I put up my guard at the slightest little thing . . .'

'I don't want to believe that you're sick.'

'Perhaps I am sick.'

'If you're worthless, I'm worthless too. If you start looking at things that way, then everyone's worthless. The Chief Security Officer, the Chief of Security, even Director-General Saitō – they're all worthless. Because the thing is, people are all like that, that's how we are. You're not an exception.'

'Maybe I'm sick.'

'Why don't you just forget everything and take a few months off?'

'I'd need a letter from a doctor, right?'

'You can get one. If you tell the doctor what you just told me, and stand by your story, he'd give you one even if you told him you didn't need it.'

'So you think I'm crazy?'

'You're not normal, that's for sure.'

'And I should take advantage of that to get a few months off?'

'What's the woman like?'

'The woman?'

'You let it slip, earlier.'

'Hmm . . .'

'This wouldn't happen to be love-sickness, would it?'

'In some ways it feels like that.'

'Man, you're such a slippery bastard!'

Tsuneo seemed unwilling to say any more, so Emoto didn't probe.

The following day, rather suddenly, it was decided that Tsuneo would take a full month off to concentrate on his treatment.

* * *

Tsuneo returned to his post toward the end of October. He wasn't as spirited as he had been in the summer, but he devoted himself seriously to his work. One evening after a night raid, when everyone was drinking at a yakitori place in Kyōbashi, Chief Security Officer Honda, who was sitting next to him at the counter, offered him a word of encouragement.

'You know, there's not a person alive who doesn't have all sorts of things to deal with. We just try to do the best we can. You're not alone.'

'Yes, sir.' Tsuneo gave a small smile and poured a little more sake into Honda's cup. 'It's true, I'm really not the only one.'

'Absolutely. Everyone's been worried about you, you know. We're all thrilled that you've managed to get your spirits up, we really are. Hey, everyone, isn't that right?' Honda shouted these last words. And all Tsuneo's colleagues called back: 'Absolutely!' 'Best thing we could have hoped for!' 'We're thrilled all right!' Everyone wanted to cheer him on. After the yakitori place they went to a bar that had karaoke and sang together until after three in the morning.

The next day, Honda went to the Chief of Security's office and told his boss how emotional the group had become.

'I'm glad to hear that,' said Chief Kamihara, nodding and smiling. 'You know, at the end of the day the people in this office are all pretty good individuals.'

'Yes, sir,' Honda agreed. 'Good individuals, every one.'

19

Early in November, Tsuneo took another day off.

He stayed in his room, waiting to hear the woman's voice.

Six months had passed since he'd last heard from her. Today was the day she had said she'd call him, one last time. Assuming she hadn't just been speaking in a general way when she said 'six months' time', it made sense to expect to hear from her on the same date half a year later. Tsuneo hadn't promised her anything, and he had no idea how her feelings might have changed since then, but seeing as she hadn't spoken to him a single time during the intervening period, he figured she too might be looking forward, to some extent, to the end of these six months.

From around the fourth month, Tsuneo had occasionally thought of calling the woman himself, instead of just waiting. He found himself thinking that maybe he had wronged her. It was his own shallowness, after all, that led him to misinterpret her reluctance to meet as ingratiating cuteness or self-pity, when in truth her hesitation had much deeper roots. He realized now that a woman so lonely that she could ignore physical realities and succeed in transmitting her voice to another human being, as she had, wouldn't feel the need to try and be flirtatious.

On the other hand, it struck him that calling her right away, while he was feeling bad about what he had done, might itself be kind of a worthless thing to do. Tsuneo couldn't imagine what about the woman might be so unbearably ugly, but if her fierce desire not to be seen was what had blocked his eyesight, as he suspected, then it hardly seemed appropriate for him to take the frivolous step of interjecting his own sentimentality into her world.

So he decided to wait the full six months, hoping she'd return. He had a hard time believing anyone could be so dreadfully ugly that no one could even bear to look at her. But then, come to think of it, he wasn't able to imagine her solitude either – to imagine what precisely her solitude consisted of. Maybe, he thought, I really don't have the slightest inkling of the depths of human reality.

He wanted to see her solitude and ugliness for himself. If they really were beyond his imagination, then surely there had to be other things of which he was equally ignorant. Perhaps there was beauty out there more stunning than he could imagine, happiness of which he couldn't even dream.

Seen from the perspective of one with a knowledge of all that, his own regrets and agonies concerning Eric would seem trite, so trivial that it would be irritating even to have to consider them.

He wanted to meet her.

He was awake at dawn. By noon, he still hadn't heard her voice. He recalled Emoto's suggestion that it might be 'lovesickness', but was too agitated even to wince at the memory. He waited, holding his breath.

He couldn't help getting hungry, though.

A little past two, he had a fairly light lunch of bread and coffee. Restless, he was just washing his cup when it happened.

'Hello.'

He heard her voice so clearly it was as if she were right
behind him.

He lifted his face.

'Finally . . .' He turned off the water. 'I was waiting!' She
wouldn't be there even if he turned around, of course, but nev-
ertheless he slowly turned to look. There was no one there.

'*My voice reached you very easily,*' said the woman calmly.

'The whole six months, I was trying to keep cool. I felt all
sorts of different things at different times, but now I regret having gotten angry at you. I apologize.'

'*It was my fault.*'

'I want you to meet with me. You said I wouldn't be strong
enough to bear it, but I'm a grown-up, I can take it. I can't
believe there are things in this world I won't even be able to
bear the sight of. I don't know, maybe there are such things. If
there are, let me see them for myself. If something happens to
me as a result, it will be my own fault. I want to know you.'

'*After today, I'll never speak to you again.*'

'No, it's fine, speak to me.'

'*I'll ruin your life.*'

'It won't be ruined.'

'*Can you fall in love? Can you marry? After hearing a voice like
this?*'

'That doesn't matter to me in the slightest.'

'*You're bound to start hating a woman who's no more than a
voice.*'

'That's why I want to meet you!'

'*This voice is my ugliness. My selfishness.*'

'What are you afraid of?'

'*Just once.*'

'Once is fine with me.'

'*Only today.*'

'You'll meet me, then?'

'*And then I'll disappear.*'

'Why do you take that attitude?'

'*I've been thinking about it for the last two months or so. I'll meet you once, then I'll disappear.*'

'You have to meet me *first*, though.'

'*Four o'clock.*'

'Four o'clock today, right?'

'*Go to the Gaienmae subway stop.*'

'I can get there easily.'

'*From Aoyama Street, walk toward the Memorial Picture Gallery.*'

'On that big road lined with ginkgo trees, right, with the wide sidewalks?'

'*Walk on the left side.*'

'Heading toward the Memorial Picture Gallery on the left?'

'*It seems a pretentious place to meet, I know, but . . .*'

'I'm sure it will be very pretty – all the yellow leaves on the ginkgo trees.'

'*I like the Memorial Picture Gallery, and it's a convenient location.*'

'I'll see you there.'

'*I'll call to you when I see you.*'

'Thank you.'

Ever so softly the sense of her presence faded.

* * *

Tsuneo prepared to go.

He couldn't deny that he felt a bit scared. Maybe he would panic and run away? Maybe he would dash off, maybe he'd hurt her again, very badly, as he had before? But at the same time, he felt excited at the possibility that he might come face to face with something he could never have imagined.

He found it hard to believe there was anything unimaginable in the environment he lived in. In present-day Japan no one felt anything, for instance, like the terror, the indifference, the egotism, the murderous rage, and the confusion that they say soldiers experienced on the battlegrounds of the Vietnam War. And yet, if he accepted what the woman had said, then even here, within the seemingly unremarkable bustle of Tokyo, there were stagnant pools of inconceivably intense solitude, sadness, and ugliness.

He took the train to Shinbashi, then switched to the subway, the Ginza line.

What if I had told people on a battleground in Vietnam the story of what happened between Eric and me? Everyone would just have smirked, I'm sure. They'd have told me, Yeah, so what? In a place where you're surrounded by nothing but violent disorder, where everywhere you look there are corpses lying on the ground, the things that took place between Eric and me would hardly even have seemed worth mentioning.

She must have felt the same way. Set alongside the realities of her own life, the confession he'd made to her must have seemed utterly insignificant.

And what *were* the realities of her life? What sort of reality could be so dreadful that it made his experience with Eric pale in comparison? Who knows, maybe I'm looking for a reality like that, maybe that's all this is. Maybe I'm just trying to find a reality extreme enough that it will make me forget Eric.

No, that's not true. At least, that's not all there is to it. I want to be overwhelmed by the depths of her emotions – to confront the inconceivable reality of her life. All the things happening around me are so flimsy, so pointless, they hardly seem worth the trouble.

He got off the subway at Gaienmae. By the time he emerged above ground, the cloudless sky was already tinged with the colors of twilight.

A gentle breeze gusted through the long rows of ginkgo trees that lined the avenue leading to the woman's favorite meeting spot, the Memorial Picture Gallery; the yellow leaves trembled, gleaming brilliantly in the sharply slanting rays of the sun. There weren't many people on the street.

If the woman was standing there waiting she should be immediately apparent, but he didn't see anyone he thought might be her. It was still a little early. Figuring he could always walk back up the road, he started heading slowly toward the gallery, just as she had instructed.

An overweight white man came jogging toward him. Hearing the sound of a bicycle behind him, he glanced back. An elderly woman, casually dressed, pedaled past with a German shepherd trotting along at her side. Both the bicycle and the dog moved off rapidly into the distance. The jogger passed by, panting. Then Tsuneo's eye spied another elderly woman, way off in the distance, walking slowly in his direction, one step at a time, as if she had to check to make sure she was okay before taking the next step.

'That's not you, is it?' he thought, looking back.

'*No*,' said the woman's voice.

There were no likely candidates behind him, either.

'*Thank you for coming such a long way.*'

'I got here a little early.'

'*I thought you might, so I came early too.*'

'I don't see anyone who looks like you.'

'*Stop walking.*'

'Okay . . .'

'*Because you have to count.*'

'Count what?'

'*Trees.*'

'Why?'

'*It's the fifth from where you are now, toward the Picture Gallery. I'm under that tree.*'

Her tone was so matter-of-fact that he felt a bit let down.

'Can I continue on now?'

'*Yes.*'

He started walking slowly forward, keeping his eye on the fifth tree. One, two. With each tree he passed, he found it harder to breathe. In his heart, he tried to smile.

'You're not going to come out until I get there?'

'*I don't have the courage.*'

'I feel as if my knees are about to give out. You've built up everything so much I feel like I might freeze. Oh, I just got a glimpse of you! You moved, didn't you? Are you wearing navy blue? A sweater?'

'*It's a cardigan. The color of grapes. And a skirt. And a white blouse.*'

'Yes, a white blouse, and –' Tsuneo broke off there, stopped walking.

The woman appeared to be staring at the bark of the tree right in front of her eyes. Then, evidently just noticing that Tsuneo was standing there, she turned her fair face toward him.

Still three or four meters away, Tsuneo held his breath. This woman was lovely. She looked as if she were under twenty.

'Ah –' Tsuneo let out something like a sigh, and nodded.

'Hi,' said the young woman. Her hair, which was fairly short, didn't appear to have been given any fancy styling, it was just cut so it was all the same length. She wore almost no make-up. Her pale, peach-colored lips were slightly parted.

'Ah . . . hi,' Tsuneo answered her, but he couldn't move. The woman's eyes weren't looking at him. They seemed to be focused a little off to the side.

'Mr Kasama?'

'Yes . . .'

Soon he realized that the girl's eyes were sightless. But . . . this wasn't her.

'Again! You're doing this to me again?' screamed Tsuneo in his heart. 'This isn't you. I can see that this girl is blind. I know from our encounter at Hibiya Park that you aren't blind. Why are you doing this? I mean, look at this girl, she's only seventeen or eighteen!'

'Should I do something?' asked the girl.

Tsuneo took a deep breath, trying to calm himself before he spoke.

'I'm sorry,' he said, his voice shaking. 'Could you wait a moment?'

'All right.' The girl nodded. She wore an expression that

made it look as if there was something she was trying to recall.

'*She's a pretty girl, isn't she?*' said the woman with the voice.

'Yes, but so what? What do you think this is going to accomplish?'

'*Tell yourself she's me.*'

'That's impossible.'

'*When you remember me, lay my voice over the form of this girl.*'

'What do you think that would accomplish?'

'*I can be pretty inside you.*'

'That's ridiculous.'

'*You'll have no other form in which to remember me. Because you haven't seen anything but her.*'

'Where are you?'

'*Don't try to find me. Just look at her. As long as I can remain in your eyes like this, in the form of a girl this lovely, I'll be able to say goodbye. I won't have to call you again.*'

'Why do something so sad?'

'*Because I love you.*'

'Cut the sweet talk. I know you're not that kind of person.'

'*I'm not being sweet.*'

'Saying you want to remain in this lovely form . . . I mean, can you get any more sentimental than that?'

'*Goodbye.*'

'No! I want to meet you! I want to know you!'

There was no answer.

'Where are you!'

He scanned his surroundings.

There was no one but the motionless girl.

'Where are you?' It was hard to scream without using his voice. But he didn't want to frighten the girl.

'I'm desperate to see you! I want to meet you!'

Shouting in his heart, he ran his gaze up and down the sidewalk across the street.

'Where are you!'

He looked up at the ginkgo trees. He turned back and looked at the cars streaming past on Aoyama Street.

'Answer me! Where are you!'

There was no reply. He listened hard.

He was so agitated he couldn't even tell whether she was there or not. He stood very still. For some time he didn't move.

'Is everything okay?' The girl tipped her head a little to one side.

'Everything's fine.' Tsuneo shook his head. He tried to smile, but couldn't.

'Well, okay. But . . .'

The girl stayed in the same spot, frozen, as if he had ordered her not to move.

Not wanting to frighten her, Tsuneo spoke. 'So,' he asked, 'why are you here anyway?' He was still standing a little distance away.

'Because I was asked to stand here,' replied the girl brightly.

'Who asked you?'

'A woman. About a month ago, when I was out taking a walk.'

'What did she say?'

'She said if I came and stood here today for about fifteen minutes, she'd give me ten thousand yen. When a man called Mr Kasama came, I had to say hello to him. That was all.'

'Didn't you find it kind of an odd request?'

'I did, but she kept telling me there was no danger, she told me that several times, and it would be daytime, and I was happy to be able to earn some money.'

'What was the woman like?'

'You can see that I'm blind, can't you?'

'I'm talking about how she seemed to you.'

'She seemed like a good person. People's voices are honest, you know.'

'I see . . .'

'Can I go now?'

'You can go. Do you need a hand?'

'No, I'm all right. I know this street. I live nearby.'

'Did you get your money?'

'I had her pay me in advance.'

The girl gave a little laugh, but her eyes didn't move. Then she started walking off toward Aoyama Street. Tsuneo gazed after her, fascinated by her every move.

'Goodbye!' said the girl.

'Ah . . . goodbye.'

The way she walked away from him, without using a stick, her feet ever so slightly turned out . . . if he hadn't already known it, he never would have guessed she was blind. And it was true, from now on whenever he thought of the woman with the voice he would remember this lovely young girl.

He watched her move further and further away, feeling as though he had been abandoned.

'Where are you?' One last time he called to the woman.

He stood there for a while, waiting, but no one answered.